Forever Yours!

♡ ♡ ♡ ♡

SONAL SINGH

Copyright © Sonal Singh

All Rights Reserved.

This book has been self-published with all reasonable efforts taken to make the material error-free by the author. No part of this book shall be used, reproduced in any manner whatsoever without written permission from the author, except in the case of brief quotations embodied in critical articles and reviews.

The Author of this book is solely responsible and liable for its content including but not limited to the views, representations, descriptions, statements, information, opinions and references ["Content"]. The Content of this book shall not constitute or be construed or deemed to reflect the opinion or expression of the Publisher. Neither the Publisher nor Editor endorse or approve the Content of this book or guarantee the reliability, accuracy or completeness of the Content published herein and do not make any representations or warranties of any kind, express or implied, including but not limited to the implied warranties of merchantability, fitness for a particular purpose. The Publisher and Editor shall not be liable whatsoever for any errors, omissions, whether such errors or omissions result from negligence, accident, or any other cause or claims for loss or damages of any kind, including without limitation, indirect or consequential loss or damage arising out of use, inability to use, or about the reliability, accuracy or sufficiency of the information contained in this book.

To those who are good, true and loyal
friend to someone.

- Teenage dream- Katy Perry
- Ziddi Dil- Vishal Dadlani
- Maahi Ve- A.R. Rehmaan
- I'll be there for you- The Rembrandts
- Ek Zindagi- Sachin Jigar, Taniska Sanghvi
- Fearless- Taylor Swift
- Khwabon ke Parinday- Alyssa Mendonsa and Mohit Chauhan

Chapter 1

Birthday sucks!

It was seven in the evening and I was swinging at the phone counter near the dining hall.

"Your birthday is coming soon. I'll try to come there and hopefully your father gets a holiday too!"

"It's okay mumma. I'll celebrate it with dadi and my friends! "

"I hope I get a holiday... okay, take care of yourself and if possible, go to dadi. She misses you, uh— I have to go now and study hard, bye!"

The call disconnected. I put the receiver of the telephone down and started walking to my room.

My mother was in the navy and my father was in army. It was impossible for my parents to get a holiday for my birthday because of their work. They both try to come together on my birthday but it literally never happened. They come and visit me at their suitable time. I barely go to my own home because I was in the senior most class and I am too lazy to do that.

As my parents are on borders which leaves me and my dadi, so I was admitted to this army boarding school.

I was the third student of our first batch. The admissions were done in sixth grade in this school.

Before me, Parul and Shree were already there. I made friends with them and till today, we are good friends. I walked with all these things rambling in the head. Suddenly, a slap landed at the back of my head.

"Ouch!" I caressed my head and turned. "What was that for?"

It was Prashant, standing at the rail bound. I was bit annoyed. Prashant was the fourth student of our batch. He came after me and was a part of our circle.

"Hello!" He had a childish charm in his voice.

"For that you hit me? You idiot!" I walked away, he tagged along.

"Why so bummed out?"

"Mumma called."

"Oh! Are they gonna come this time?"

My friends knew about this from the start. Well, we all had the same scenario.

"They say they will try but...you know it never happens!"

"Get cheered up, you can't sulk about this. We are the upcoming generation of armed services!" He flexed his muscles. A sigh escaped from my lips.

"Why you were here?"

"Nothing! My relative sister got admitted so I was here to check on her." I nodded.

"I am going upstairs. See you at dinner! "

"It won't bother me if you don't come to dinner." He stuck his tongue out.

"Bleh!" I climbed the stairs.

I banged against the door of my room, and it swung. Parul was there, reading stories.

"How was your call?" She didn't look up.

"Regular as always!" I left my body at the edge of the bed and fell on the mattress.

"Aren't they gonna come?"

"What do you think?" I rolled over.

"They will try but won't make it...something like that!" Her eyes were rolling.

"That's what happened but you know I can't sulk about it... well! It's been a while, I should go and visit dadi."

"Hmm, what's for dinner?" her eyes were buried into the pages.

I lowered my gaze to her and shrugged.

"I'll find it by, myself." She pushed herself away.

She stood up and closed the door behind her. I straightened my spine on the bed and closed my eyes. Unknowingly, days of my tenth birthday flashed. It was the birthday which was celebrated before coming here and mumma and papa and dadi, everyone was there.

I was so happy that day. Even Mahi was there too. Mahi was my childhood best friend and used to live in neighbour house. That was the last party that I had with my parents.

It was such a happy memory but sometimes fate plays different cards. That day brings me some bitter memories. After a couple of days of my birthday, Mahi was found dead in front of her house. Police concluded that Mahi was on the roof and lost her balance while sitting on the rail bound.

My heart was shattered into thousand pieces. I didn't cry for two days but on the third day, I found our picture with my first broken tooth. We lost our teeth nearly at the same time. It was a picture where we were laughing together. I had my tooth in my hand and she was pointing to the window between her teeth.

My little heart couldn't hold the amount of tears which were collected inside.

It was her father who took that photograph. After this accident, they moved away and I was sent here.

"Come on, it's *chole*!" It was Parul who screamed as she stormed in. I opened my eyes with a jerk.

"You…You will kill me someday." I patted my heart.

"If I got the opportunity, yes! …now come."

She dragged me down the stairs, barged into the dining hall and lined up for the plates. I followed her. She took two full spoons of *chole*. We sat on the table. Prashant joined us.

"Look, the void has sat to eat!" He pointed at Parul.

She glared at him. "Do you want to die?"

"No! But if you eat that much, you are definitely gonna die!"

She gave him a look. Prashant teasingly took a bite from his plate.

"Go to hell!" She stuck her tongue out on him and resumed eating.

"That's what people say when they can't find a comeback!"

Prashant always teased her and so did Parul. They were the Tom and Jerry of their class. They were in different section then me.

"When is the monthly test?" I asked Prashant.

"Probably around the twentieth of this month or next."

"Have you studied?"

"Not even a word!"

"Same *yaar!*"

"I'll cheat from her paper." Prashant clicked his tongue.

"Hehe, like I'll let you! Loser!"

"The loser is calling herself!"

I was looking at them and was actually getting entertained while having dinner. At the start we used to complain about not having the TV here but, I got some show to enjoy!

Suddenly, my eyes landed at the gate of the dining hall.

A boy entered which attracted my attention. He had wheat skin and his black hair were fighting to settle down. He was a bit tall, actually taller than me. His lips were perfectly aligned and pressed against each other. He was in a full sleeved light grey hood.

I saw him lining up at the counter. He walked across me. He had pretty eyes and long eyelashes. I found myself staring at him. He saw me and then he rolled his eyes away. He walked and sat on the seat far away. I just embarrassed myself, what was I doing? I banged my head with my palm.

"What happened?" It was Parul.

"Um... nothing... just...chewed chilly!" I lied, a lame lie.

"Oh! But...leave it!" They resumed their teasing fight.

What the hell? What the hell just happened?

"Hey, do you guys wanna go out for fun?" Prashant took a bite.

The day after tomorrow was the first Sunday of the month, we were free to go for outing.

"Where?" Parul buried her spoon in the chole.

"Some place nice! Fun city, forest, fort! Wherever we mutually decide! "

"I am in! What about you?" Parul shook me.

"What? Oh... yea, fun city. I suggest!" I ate a bite.

"I am thinking of the fun city too!" Prashant ate his last bite.

"If everyone agrees, I'll be there!" Parul gulped.

"I am done!" Prashant threw his spoon in the dish and stood up.

"Where are you going?" I stopped him.

"Outside! For a walk. "

"Liar! Shefali is outside." Parul gave her a look.

"Well in that case! Hurry, go!" I mocked him.

Shefali was a girl who had cute looks and her mother was in the navy. She was more interested in painting and art than building strategy or fighting. She was knowledgeable but used to be quiet. *Quiet people are always dangerous.* You never know what kind of weapon they have on their sleeve!

Prashant had liking towards her. Prashant took his plate and went to the sink area.

"I need more *chole*. I am going!" I stood up and took my plate to fill my bowl.

There were other junior girls in line. They gave me a pace to scoop the gravy. They were talking in a low voice.

"She never had any issues with anyone!" They were three in the group.

"Maybe it's a boy matter!" A girl with glasses said it.

"But that doesn't explain it!" The first one corrected her.

"Some say it's an animal who came from the nearby forest area!" The third one gave her theory.

I was listening to them keenly. I retraced my steps and came back to the seat.

They were talking about the incident which took place two days ago. A girl of junior class was found dead at the lobby. Everyone says that the girl fell from the roof by accident but it doesn't explain why her body was half eaten?

"Well, the girls over there were saying it was an animal!"

"And who taught that animal to throw a dead body out of the roof? And one more thing, the nearby forest is safe. We have been going there since we came here. Each and every training has been done there, have you ever spotted an animal? "

"No one knows about the deep area?"

"I know, there is nothing, it's just that the deep area had so many swamps. That's why we are not allowed to go there!"

"Who told you?"

"Our trainer boy, who tails behind the PE teacher!"

"And why did he tell you?" I raised my brows.

"Because...I was stubborn to know and we are good acquaintances!"

"I see!" I playfully hit her by my elbow.

"I am done!" I put the spoon on the plate.

After a few minutes, she was done too. I begged her to put my plate to the sink because I didn't want to. I was on the table, waiting for her.

I saw him, again, but he was looking at me with his cold gaze. I rolled my eyes away from him.

"Woah! Who is he?" Parul appeared.

"I don't know."

"He looks good!"

"So?

"Nothing! Let's go out...hm!"

I took her hand and went outside of the building. The air was fresh and a bit cold but it felt nice. The breeze swept through my hair. The charcoaled path was clean and nice. A lot of students were strolling over there. I could spot Prashant looking at Shefali. I scoffed.

"This person is unbelievable!" Parul commented from behind.

"Leave him, right now he is mad in love!" I double quoted it.

We walked around the campus and came across the school. My eyes went to the roof.

A roof accident!

A shiver ran through my body, leaving me with the hint of sadness.

"What'd you think? What could've happened?" She was looking around.

"I don't wanna talk about depressing things, I am already depressed!" I scratched the back of my head.

"Are you listening?" I hit her.

"I am trying to find that guy!"

"Who?"

"That nice looking guy from the dinner hall."

"Leave that guy!"

After talking and chatting around a while, the clock hit the curfew time.

"I didn't find!" Parul pouted.

"Aww!" I patted her head. "Let's go! We'll find him tomorrow."

We locked our hands and swung them and walked towards our rooms. She lived across from my room on the second floor.

"Nighty-night." I went inside and fell on my bed.

The neon lamp on my desk was lit.

The blanket was folded, I spread it on the bed and slipped under it. The lamp was still lit in the room, I was habitual of it.

A very long bell rang!!!! Annoying! I stretched my hands to the side table and stopped the alarm. It's five in the morning, and the roll call will start in an hour. The PE teacher won't let me go away this time. This month, I've been late three times because I overslept. That oversleeping thing wasn't my fault, I've been a hyperactive kid from the start. It's just I experience nightmares occasionally. They seem too real and their after effect makes me too dizzy.

I stood up from my bed and went to the bathroom to brush my teeth. I put on my track suit and shoes and knocked over Parul's door. She was tying her shoes. A lot of students were already on the ground. She locked her door and we both rushed down.

The black tracksuit was gleaming on the green grass. In a few minutes, everyone from the batch was lined up. Other classes were on their assigned ground. Soon the PE teacher came with his whistle.

"Students, take one hand distance from all sides!" He screamed with his half strength but his voice echoed in the ground.

We all took one hand distance and soon we all were spread uniformly. Parul was behind me. The roll call started. Unintentionally my eyes went from one to another as they raised their hands and called out the number. My turn came, I was 26 on the ground. I raised my hand and spoke my number but still my eyes were roaming.

"27!" I heard it.

The voice was heavy, so heavy that it would drew everyone's attention but it left me in confusion. That spot was vacant from a while. I saw someone standing there but didn't had a moment to look who it is? I turned my head, it was him. The guy whom I saw in the dining room yesterday. He saw me too but he gave me a cold look. I felt insulted, so I turned my head back. The roll call ended at 30. The warm up and basic exercise started. After twenty minutes of exercise, PE whistled.

"Follow us in the pair of lines!" Then he took the lead.

First half of students went up first and then the second half did, he was running beside me and it was eating me from inside. Somehow I managed to run three kilometres along him. Everyone reached the target flag in the forest. The whistle blew.

"Students! Now use your strength and climb up this little mountain. Let's meet at the top! "

He blew the whistle again and gestured for everyone to run. It was a daily routine, we were doing this from day one except for the fact that we did it on different mountains.

That forest had lot of mountains and it was for cardio but sometimes we used to wander here for fun!

Parul and I were alongside. I left his side when I started climbing on the mountain. It was a slanted mountain so it was a bit easy to climb on it if you align yourself with the slope. In ten minutes, I was on the top and so were other students. We all sat down there to get some breath. Soon the morning broke out and we saw the sunrise. We witness it every morning but still cannot get enough of this ethereal sight. I sat down with my legs in front. Prashant joined us. He was 29 on the ground. The air was refreshing. The first ray of sunlight hit the ground. I inhaled a long, fresh breath.

I was coping with my breath.

"Where were Nikhil and Shree last night?" I sighed.

"They were with Pathak Sir, probably working on upcoming investiture."

"Ya! That guy was standing at 8 o'clock. Ha, I couldn't get enough look but you scored! He was beside you. His voice, my god! I am leaving my body..." Parul whispered in my ear.

"Don't you think you are looking over that guy way too much?"

"You won't know babe! What is the feeling of being in love? Ah!" She covered her mouth. I gazed at her. She was a drama queen and everyone knew it!

"It's not love but I do like looking at him. It just refreshes my mind! "

"You are talking like he is your antidote for living!"

"Something like that!"

"It's nothing serious but... yea! Don't judge, it's just my heart who keeps liking handsome boys! "

"Ain't I handsome?" Prashant heard it.

"Ya! Go and ask your Shefali!" Parul nearly screamed.

"You little..." Prashant gritted but was interrupted.

The PE was on the top of the mountain and whistled.

"Students! Assemble yourself! "

We had to stand according to our numbers. Soon the roll call started, he was standing beside me.

Again! And he will, every day!

After the roll call we were instructed to run back to the ground. On the ground we did final routine of exercise.

After the exercise, we were dismissed. We all were sweaty. Everyone jogged to their buildings.

I reached to my room and stripped all of my clothes. After a cold shower, I relaxed myself by throwing myself on the bed. After ten minutes, I got dressed for school. Knee length black skirt and white shirt tucked in with white striped tie and black blazer. The blazer was thin. It worked as a vest for us. My short hair were tied in an open ponytail. I buckled up my shoes with long white socks. The school bag was already on the desk. A knock was there on the door. I knew who it was, Parul. I opened the door, she was there with her bag and all ready.

"Let's go!"

"One second!" I went to my desk and picked up my bag and locked the door.

We both went down. We had to walk for a kilometre to the school. The buildings and school were distant but before that, our breakfast was waiting. We put our bags at the front counter of the building and went to the hall. As I walked in, I saw him, 27! He was sitting in the front row. Parul could not hold her mouth.

"Oh my god! He is right there, the universe is conspiring for us! "

I held her tightly and took her to the meal counter.

"Yea, I hope you both eat in single plate one day." I commented.

"I am looking forward to it!" She winked.

We sat down and soon Prashant joined us.

"What's the smell?" He sniffed.

"What smell?" I sniffed too.

"I think Parul hasn't bathed!" He closed his nostrils.

"I think you are sniffing yourself!"

"Shut up! You both stink." I made my final decision.

"Okay but you are stinky too!" Parul sipped the glass.

I shot her a look.

We finished our breakfast and headed towards the school with our bags.

Today I had only classes, no labs!

We reached the gate of our school. Our class was on second floor, in the senior section. We took our turn to the senior section and climbed the floor. On the notice board, a new notice was tagged.

"What's that?" I asked Prashant.

"Ah! Remember three days ago, about that girl! Because of that accident, it's restricted to go up to the terrace! "

"It was restricted before too!" Parul said in between.

"But this time, it's serious!"

We were talking about things and walked inside the classrooms. I walked to my seat, the brown single desk of mine was waiting for me. I slid my bag under the table and put the bottle in the stand then we went to their classroom while talking.

Soon the assembly started and ended with national anthem. We marched to our classes.

"Hey! Sara, good morning! "

"Morning!" It was Aarya.

"Today Vijay sir will give us the chemistry project, have you decided with whom you will team up?"

"Ah... no! I hate chemistry and I hate chemistry projects!" I nearly cried.

"I've heard that this time sir will decide the pair! I hope I get paired up with him!" She pointed across to me. I looked in the direction, it was 27.

Aargh!

My world collapsed and got dissolved into the black hole. It's not even twenty four hours and we are not on good note and he is in my section! How could I possibly bear him in the same room?

"He is in our section!" I kind of screamed because I was taken aback. He saw me.

"You know him?" I turned my face quickly!

"No...But I saw him at the dinner and he is my squadron! "

"Oh...well, we don't know about the chemistry but in physics, you are already mine! I am going over there." She winked and left my table.

My head was resting in my palms as I was trying to digest this brand new information. He is in my section!

HE IS IN MY SECTION!

I drank water out of my bottle, and then the first bell rang. Vijay sir, our chemistry teacher came in.

"Good morning students!"

"Good morning sir!" He was our classroom teacher too.

"So students, are you excited about the project?"

"No!" I mumbled but everyone else said yes in unison.

"I think there is one person who is not happy and that is Sara! Miss Sara, please stand up!" For some reason, I am always on his target.

I stood up, preparing myself for the upcoming insult.

"So Miss Sara, tell me with whom you wanna pair up because you have to do the project?"

"I am ..."

"Before that..." He cut me in the middle, *first blow!*

"Before Miss Sara says something, I would like to introduce a new student to the class. Please come here!" Sir called him in front of the board and all this while I was getting the whole celebrity vibe.

"Introduce yourself!" Sir told him.

I was standing in his perfect line of sight, he saw me first and then took away his gaze.

"Hello! I am Siddharth Kayega. I am transferred here from the sister school." His heavy voice fell on my eardrums.

"Okay Siddharth, now tell me your recent chemistry test marks?" Mr. Vijay was preparing the stage for my next insult.

"Forty nine out of fifty!" He said firmly but carelessly and that will be the second blow of insult for me.

"That's a pretty good score, isn't it? Sara!" I could not feel more annoyed.

"Yes sir!"

"Well as he is our new student and is very good at chemistry so Sara, I have decided that you will pair up with him." He put pressure on the word good but my pressure shifted on us being a pair. I wasn't feeling anything and my senses just stopped working for a moment.

My soul fell into the bottomless pit and denied to ever come back.

"I have already paired with someone!" I had to lie and I was good at it.

"Who?"

"Aarya!" I couldn't think of anyone else.

"Yea, average grader and below average grader! Wow! I want this year's project to be fantastic because they all will be exhibited at the joint event so I cannot bear any project with no perfection and— students, this time I have paired up everyone and I will announce the names. Sara, you will pair up with him, now sit down!" That was a rude force.

I had to do this project with him, no choice! It's do or die. I sat down and looked at him. He was looking in front, his was face was pissing me off. I gritted my teeth at him and at that moment, he turned his head. He saw me. I quickly buried my face in the table.

Vijay sir was announcing the pairs of the project. I didn't know how I would converse with him and he doesn't even like me. His cold eyes always remind me of that. The class went on with the chapters and I didn't move my neck a bit. I don't wanna see him. After a tiring hour, the class ended. Before leaving the class, Vijay sir made the last announcement.

"The pairs should teach each other and discuss. I want each and every child to be familiar with their own project concept and you people are free to choose the topic but ask about it to me for once." Then he left. I couldn't hate this teacher or this subject anymore!

I was standing at my hating limit that all of my hate ran out. I looked at him slowly, he was looking at me and caught my gaze. I quickly turned my head and started to see somewhere else.

Class after class till lunch! Finally, bell for the lunch rang. I came out of the class, Parul was outside her class with Prashant. They saw me, I waved at them. They both came running towards me.

"Shree and Nikhil should be here!"

Soon Nikhil and Shree came out of their class.

"I didn't see you guys for a very long time." Prashant dramatically leaned on them.

"Let's go!" Nikhil hooked onto my neck.

Nikhil and I were good friends, like very good friends. We knew each other's story and past life. He had a normal family. We always talked about our dreams, how he wants to become an officer in army and how I wanted to become a pilot in air-force.

Nikhil was a kind of school crush. Girls of our batch and other junior batches used to like him. He was always calm and collected. Before going for the lunch, Shree was running a little late so we waited.

We were at the fountain of the school.

Suddenly I felt some water on me. Prashant threw water at Parul. They were running wild. Nikhil was beside me, suddenly he threw water at me from his cupped hands.

I dodged but still got some on me. He ran away, I also filled my hand and ran but the water got spilled on Parul so she tried to soak me up and then Prashant poured little bit more and then Shree came out and got involved.

Soon a water fight started.

We were just running around in that area. We were already half soaked. There was someone's bottle, I picked it and threw it over to Nikhil. It had enough water.

The water from the bottle flew at him and damn to his reflexes, he sensed it and ducked. He avoided it and the water went behind him. I looked at him, the water had gotten on someone. I lifted my face, it was 27. His face was wet and so was his blazer. Nikhil stood up and looked at me. I was in shock. Why on earth did this happen? The water was dripping down from his face and went down to his chiselled jawline and then got on the gravel ground.

I hate it. Why is he so good looking?

"I... I... I am really sorry!" I was stuttering.

He wiped his face with his bare hands and opened his eyes. Disappointment in his eyes was clear. He unbuttoned his blazer and hung it on his hand.

"Sorry brother!" Nikhil came to my rescue.

"It's alright!"

He gave a solid glare, a glare with the warning that if this was not school, he would've killed me! He walked with water dripping from his forehead.

"I am really sorry... I'm really sorry!" I screamed behind him, he didn't turn.

"I am sorry! I hope you are not mad!" I was still screaming. I guess he could not listen to me anymore.

"It's okay, it was a mistake. You didn't mean to do that." Nikhil patted my shoulder.

"But the mistake happened so I should apologize!"

He chuckled. "He is not listening anymore and— you don't have to go. By the way, who is he? "

"He is a transferred student. He is in my section, he joined today. "

"Hmm… and on his first day, you gave him a sun kissed water bath!"

"It's all your fault! You shouldn't have ducked!" I hit him on his arm.

"Oh come on! You missed the shot and it's all my fault?
"

"Yes!"

"Hmm, okay! It was my fault but can we go for lunch. I am hungry!"

He dragged me to the hall. Everyone was already there, soaked! We were in line for fried rice.

As I sat down on the table, it turn out I was really hungry, especially after the insult in chemistry class.

I narrated the whole incident of chemistry class to them. They laughed too hard that Shree choked on rice. Soon the laughter settled down.

"Oh yeah! I wanted to ask this to both of you, Nikhil and Shree! Where do you wanna go tomorrow?" The next day was Sunday.

"I don't know! Any suggestions?" Shree took a bite.

"What about fun city? Sara wants to go there!" Parul licked the spoon.

"Nice! I am in." Shree clapped hands.

"If everyone is going there then I am there too!" Nikhil adjusted his sleeve.

"Then it's done, tomorrow we all are going to a fun city!" Prashant stood up.

"Control!" Parul pulled him down.

Everyone resumed eating and was talking about stuff. My mind was thinking something but I didn't know what I was thinking.

"Hey! What are you thinking about?" Parul clicked on my plate.

"I don't know." My brain was working again.

"Then it's fine." Shree was getting on my nerves.

"Did you guys get the projects?" Parul was picking up the tomatoes.

"No, maybe in the second half!" Nikhil said.

"I got paired up but didn't chose the project."

"With whom?"

"With the guy to whom I just gave sun-kissed bath!" I plastered a smile.

Nikhil burst out in laughing and so did others.

"Seriously!" Prashant exhaled.

"Really!" Parul nearly screamed.

"Who he actually is?" Shree asked.

"A very handsome boy to whom I got a crush on!" Parul winked. Everyone wooed but Shree had different look.

Shree liked Parul.

"He is Siddharth, transferred from sister school. Chemistry topper so I am paired with him in the chemistry project plus. He is my batch and our squadron!" Parul and I exchanged glances.

"Your brilliant chemistry knowledge did all this. I can understand." Nikhil laughed.

"Stop rubbing salt on my wounds! I hate that guy! "

"Why?" Parul was in a bit of shock.

"Because he is a chemistry scholar!"

"'It' alright, you are going to be fine." Shree sympathized.

The hell I will!

Soon the meal finished and everyone went out. The lunch time got over and we all had to head back to classes.

I was the only one in a different section. We were assigned classes according to the random number we picked from the bowl while the admission process.

It felt like Harry Potter to me back then. In reality, it was!

I was little back then, if I knew, I would have picked the same number as Parul.

This time it was an English lecture. Kind of music and it doesn't involve much brain work. Soon the teacher came in and ranted about some poet. Next was Physics, my favourite! The teacher came in. The topic was electromagnetic induction. My mind was totally focused on the magnetism that I didn't think or look at him. The class was about to end, so Mr. Varun announced some topics for the project and asked us to choose whatever we liked. Everything was fine till this point but I fell into a deep hole after this moment, when Mr. Varun announced that he will not pair again so the chemistry pairs will work on the physics project too.

A spark of hate for this teacher just bloomed!

I looked at him in disappointment, he was looking at me too.

Argh!

Today God is playing with me, well played! I was clapping on my luck.

At mid noon the school dispersed, I saw him rolling his eyes at me. *What the...!*

I scoffed. He needs to be taught!

He was a fast walker, he kind of went ahead. Parul and Nikhil were outside of my class waiting for me. I took my bag and rushed out.

"Wait for me near the tree!" I was in a rush.

They didn't understand but didn't ask anything. 'Near the tree' was a famous slang used around the school. There was an old oak tree in the middle of the entire campus. It was enormous and a landmark so everyone knew where to meet.

I rushed across them and caught him in the middle of the stairs. *I wonder why he was taking stairs of other side?*

"Why did you roll your eyes at me?" *I pointed my finger at me.*

"Excuse me!"

"I saw you, mocking at me with your eyes!"

"Wake up from your little dream."

"I saw that and you know it. I know, you hate me!"

He sighed. "What do you want me to do?"

"Don't ever roll your eyes at me again!"

"As you say!" He plastered a smile and walked away.

"I hate you!" I screamed behind his back. *Bastard!*

I stomped back and went straight to the tree where Nikhil and Parul were standing.

"Don't ever talk about that guy in front of me." I roared at Parul.

"What happened?"

"I don't want to talk about it. It will just ruin my mood!"

"Well....whatever it was, let that thing go! Tomorrow we are going to a fun city! "

"Yeah!" Parul supported Nikhil.

We all walked to our building. We talked a bit over there.

"Have a rest! Let's meet in the evening and don't be such an angry bird." I nodded and then everybody went to their rooms.

Parul was walking beside me, I could see that she was curious about what happened exactly? We reached our rooms.

"Are you okay?" Parul unlocked her room.

"Yeah... I guess! "

"What happened back there?"

"Nothing... we just fought! He rolled his eyes at me!"

"Did he shout at you?" Her eyes were enlarged in question.

"No...he just mocked in low voice!"

"Oh!" She lowered her head.

"I wonder what kind of a boy he is. He seems nice, but as you told me, he is a bit savage! Aren't these guys found in books?" She was being dreamy. A scoff came out.

"In books? Like him? Don't insult books. You really have high expectations from that high class bastard? Don't you! "

"Yeah!" She exhaled "He is kind of dreamy!"

I glared at her. "You are gone case!"

I slammed the door at her face.

Chapter-2

Next day after the morning physical routine was followed with 'him' beside me. *I wish I could kill him!*

We were all ready for our little fun at the fun city. We all board the bus in our uniforms. After half an hour we were dropped near the fun city. Being a student gets you discount everywhere!

We all went to the fifth floor of the Marvel building which had the fun city. We got our gaming cards ready and then surfed through the games. We spent our first hour on air hockey. I always liked this game, I don't know why? Then car racing games and then went for virtual hunting.

I killed two deer and a bull but Prashant killed the lion so he was the winner. We spent nearly three hours there, we had to head back till five. For fun we went to the horror house. Parul used to be afraid of creepy and ghostly things. She refused to go but I dragged her in.

Scream, scream everywhere!

No doubt, it was Parul. She nearly ripped my eardrums. A ghost cosplay emerged from the cupboard from my side. My reflexes! I slapped that person in a sudden reaction. A lot of webs and skeletons hung in our way but after some time we made it to the end and came out. Parul was still in shock.

"What the hell Sara, you slapped that ghost?" Nikhil was laughing.

"I don't know why?" We all were laughing.

"Parul did only aaaaaaaaaaaaaaaaaa!" Prashant was laughing.

"Don't tease her, she's already in shock!" Shree defended.

I looked at Nikhil and he looked at me. A little giggle burst out. We sat down on a bench to cope up with breaths which ran out while laughing. We all were there for a couple of minutes, drank some water and came to our senses.

"We have around an hour! Let's play escape room and then we will eat something, okay?" Nikhil was standing.

"You laughed at me in the horror house now I will laugh at you all in the escape room!" Parul threatened us, we all looked at each other and laughter burst out in unison.

We all walked slowly to our way to escape room. It was in the end of the corridor as it needed the biggest space.

"Where is Parul?" Shree noticed.

"She went to the bathroom, she'll be back in a minute!"

"I had to go too!" I stomped.

"Let's go!" Parul came jumping.

"Well people! Head in. I'll be back in a minute. "

"Where are you going?" Parul asked.

"Where you went before!" I went away.

I found the washroom sign and went in. After washing my hands, I started to walk at the end of the corridor.

Suddenly my head hurt! An intense and excruciating pain inside my brain. My vision went blurry. I held the wall but after a few seconds the pain vanished.

That was strange! I looked in front, something was different. There was not even a single soul. The lights over my head flickered a little. My brain told me to keep walking but my guts were telling me not to and my other senses already went numb.

I came to a door. 'Room No. 4' was written on it.

I held the doorknob and circled it, opening it in the hope of finding Nikhil and others. My senses were coming back. Senses were hammering inside the wall of my brain, I could feel it.

Something wasn't right!

My head started to work again but before I could realize, I was in the room with the closed doors. The room had no lights except for a dim bulb which lit in the adjacent partition and little light from the window was falling on me.

Leave! Sara, you need to leave!

Something was about to happen, my intuitions were screaming at me. If something bad happens, I will be playing escape room in real means!

I went to the door and held the knob.

"What is the hurry sweetie?" A forced sweet but hoarse female voice came from behind.

I turned in curiosity but a smidge of fear clutched me. I couldn't see anyone but a figure, a female silhouette. Open hair, abnormal height and had her one leg on something, oh wait! *Is that a corpse?*

"Wh... who are you?" A clear shiver and stutter could be heard in my voice but I strengthen my guts.

"Does it matter? But if you are asking me, I must tell you. You do have the right to know it in your last moments."

"Last moments?" Sweat bead streaked down from my forehead.

An abnormal laugh in response. It wasn't humane.

"Yes sweetie, last moments but your strong scent...ah! I think I have to cut it down to a moment! "

"W...what? Who are you, tell me?" I was scared and was shouting. My knob in my hands wasn't opening but my hope wasn't letting it go.

"Well! What you humans say us? Demons? Monsters? Human-eater?" Again a crazy laugh.

I looked at my palm, there was blood. Blood was on the knob.

Help! It was the only thing I could, scream! Every bit of strength I've ever had, I used it all and cried for help. She laughed crazily.

"Your flesh will be cake but your scent... ah! Will be cream! "

I saw her taking steps towards me in that cracked darkness. I screamed with everything and covered my head and prayed to god! I was on my knees, coiling.

Swish, a sound!

A clear sound. Magnetic enough to force anyone to open their eyes.

I opened my eyes slowly. I saw someone. Who? I don't know, I could only see the silhouette. The silhouette was standing firm with a sword in hand.

Why there are no faces, only silhouettes?

That creature, her head was rolling on the floor and soon her body and her head turned into ashes. I saw the ashes in that dim light. The silhouette was still standing, looking at me, I could tell that. I was horror stricken so nothing came out of my mouth.

The silhouette walked towards me, slowly!

Suddenly an intense light flashed in front of my eyes that totally blinded me! Out of nowhere I felt a push between my brows.

Then, nothing!

Water splash, someone is calling my name! I came to my senses and opened my eyes. There was too much light, my eyes got squinted!

"Sara! Are you alright?" Nikhil was by my head.

"Yeah, I am alright!" Nikhil helped me sit up.

"What happened?" Prashant asked.

"What happened?" I was confused.

"I am asking you, why you were faint?"

"I was faint?"

"Did you hit your head?" Parul came forward.

"I don't know!" I seem like a mental patient.

"You were unconscious at the other end of the corridor, what were you doing over there? When you didn't come for the next five minutes we searched for you and Nikhil found you unconscious in the corridor!" Shree was nearly shouting at me.

"Really?" It was all out of range for me, I couldn't remember.

"You sure hit your head!" Prashant sat back.

"No I didn't, it's not hurting! Or... maybe I did, I can't tell."

"Let it go! We found her safe and sound, that's it. I'll get you checked at the infirmary." Nikhil helped me to stand up.

"She is safe but not sound!" Prashant was in on its own joke.

"Let's skip escape room. We'll eat and head back!" Parul helped me.

We went to the food court. Shree brought sandwiches for everyone. Everyone dug in, Nikhil handed me a sandwich.

"Are you alright?" He took a bite.

"Yeah! I think I am."

"Um...what was the last game we played?"

"Virtual hunting and then we went to horror house!"
"And after that?"

"...There is no record, here!" I tapped at my forehead.

I tried to think but I really couldn't think or remember anything. There was this gap between my memory and this gap was eating me. I finished my sandwich, even though I didn't want to. After eating. We walked to the bus stop, Nikhil was walking by my side. I was trying to find those lost five minute memories in my brain. I exhaled.

"Don't pressure yourself! It's okay if you don't remember." Nikhil read my expression.

We reached the school on time.

"Guys, I am taking her to infirmary." Everyone nodded and went to their buildings.

Infirmary was inside the school corridor so the school main gate was never latched. Only rooms were latched from outside. When we went there, Miss Nina, the female doctor of the infirmary, saw me.

"Oh Sara! Are you alright? "

"Almost." I sat on the stretcher.

"Oh! Nikhil! Please step out." Nikhil left the room.

She checked my hand by pressing some points. She stretched my legs and examined. There was no injury.

"There are no physical injuries or wounds. You are alright. Nikhil you can come in." She called out for him.

"Sara, if you feel tired, sleep tight and sound. Body will recover itself." I nodded.

Nikhil walked me out.

"I forgot about the memory thing!" I remembered.

"No need to tell anyone." He held my wrist.

"Why? She is a doctor. At least I can tell her. "

"And what will you say?"

"Um...I cannot remember!"

"Idiot, walk straight." He exhaled.

"Nikhil! What do you think? What has happened to my brain?" We started walking to the building.

"Um... as much as I've read and I have information, I can say that you had a concussion. A part of your head was hit and just because of that, you lost a part of your memory because your brain didn't want to store it or maybe it was too insignificant to remember. "

"Nice explanation. After this, I will stop thinking about it." I chuckled.

"Yeah you should stop, who knows how much memory you will lose after that."

I gave him a look. I went to hit him but he ran away. He was faster than me. I was behind him and suddenly I bumped into someone. My left side hit the ground and so did my head. This time, I really hit my head. The elbow was brazed. I looked at the person, it was 27!

Argh!

"Are you blind?" He brushed the dust.

"I think you are blind!" Anger surfaced as I saw him.

"You are the one who bumped into me!"

"I bumped, I accept! Couldn't you look? "

"What happened?" Nikhil came back.

"This blind collided with me!" He saw him.

"I am sorry from her side!"

"Hey! It was not my fault, it was his. Why are you saying sorry, take your sorry back! "

"Don't fight! You already have grown a big bump on your head, let's go to infirmary again! "

He held me by my shoulders and led me to the infirmary. This time, Miss Nina got work. She put on ointment. It was hurting.

"Just a minute ago you left and you are back! You know Sara, you are the only student whom I've treated this much."

"Then... will I get special treatment?"

"Ha-ha, very funny! Now take care of your head and here, take this ointment. Apply it regularly."

"Thank you Miss Nina!"

We walked and this time he didn't say anything. We reached my building.

"Sara, are you alright or you lost another piece of memory?"

"Enough with memory jokes!"

"Okay, okay but tell me are you really okay?"

"I guess." I felt the bump, it was really noticeable.

"Why did you say sorry to him? It was his fault! "

"It's okay Sara, saying sorry doesn't make me short."

"But still!"

"Okay, now go. I'll meet you at dinner."

He went away and I walked to the building.

I went to my room, changed into pyjamas and knocked Parul's door. She opened the door and looked at me.

"What is that?"

"A hen, I think!" I barged into the room.

"How did you hurt your head?"

"That high class bastard, we crashed into each other!" I gritted my teeth.

"Really?" She had a smile on her face.

"I wish you were in my place."

"Well, do you remember now what happened to you in the fun city?"

"No... and I am not thinking about it anymore. Nikhil said it might be a concussion, that's why I don't remember. "

"Hmm... might be. Still, you hit your head, lie down until then I'll complete this part of the book. "

"Fine!" I drew a pillow and laid straight.

Scream!! Ha! My eyes opened. A nightmare again. My lungs ran out of oxygen. It was not the first time I am experiencing these, I have been a regular customer from birth but after moving here, their frequency increased a bit. I never told anyone about this except Nikhil because he says he also dreams of frequent nightmares. Balcony would be a nice place for me right now!

"Sara!" Parul was at the door.

"Yea! I am on the balcony." She came in.

"What are you doing here?"

"Breathing!"

"Nice."

We started talking about some random stuff. We didn't realize that it was already evening.

"Let's go for dinner."

We walked to the dining hall.

Soon the boys walked in and joined us.

"Hey bumpy!" It was Nikhil.

I paused for a while. That was something I didn't think I'd ever be called.

"Bumpy?" I frowned.

"Doesn't it suit?" Nikhil clicked Shree.

"It suits her perfectly!" He gave an OK gesture.

"Bite your tongue!" I stared at them.

"When are you going to meet your dadi? " Parul broke my stare.

"I'll ask for permission tomorrow."

After school, I was going to ask for permission and if granted I'll meet dadi.

Next morning, I put some ointment on the bump. It was worse than yesterday.

It was noticeable, it was swollen.

Damn that bastard! With a swollen head, I went for the morning routine. We were on the ground with our batch, 27 was standing beside me. The PE teacher came for a quick inspection, he saw me.

"Cadet 26, what happened to your head?" I fell into an abyss and never hit the bottom.

"I hit my head, sir!" We were cadets on the ground and had to answer like that. No one dared to turn their head.

"How?" I held my breath for a while.

"I bumped into the cupboard sir!" *The culprit is standing beside me.*

"Are you well, cadet?"

"Yes sir!"

Then he walked away. The blood was boiling and anger was getting cooked. Everyone is going to laugh in class. If I could, I would've beaten 27 there.

After the routine, we went to school. After the assembly, Aarya jumped towards me.

"Hey cadet 26!" She imitated the PE trainer.

"Yes ma'am?"

"Did you really hit your head in the cupboard?" She was in other squadron but others must've told her.

"Yeah!" I went to my table.

"He shouldn't have asked you that."

"Is there anything I could do about that?" She giggled.

"Sara, will you come to the library at four? I need to solve some physics questions. "

"Sure."

"Okay then, see ya!"

I put my bag on the table but then saw something. A note! I picked it.

Chemistry project: Rusting

Physics project: Newton's cradle

PS: I don't hate you!

Who the... 27! *What a great joke to get the day started!*

I don't hate you, I imitated him. Ha-ha-ha then what? Do you like me?

In the heat of the moment, I wrote it in the paper. I crumbled it and pointed at him, he was looking in front. I can hit him, just for once. Please god!

I threw the paper ball behind his ear but... that guy was with abnormal qualities! He held the paper near his ear. I so wanted to hit him, argh! He unfolded the paper and read and wrote something back. He threw it again at me, I caught it.

No, I don't like you either! You don't exist for me.

Burn! Burn! This was on rewind in the back of my head. You got totally burnt Sara, such an insult! Incredible! I looked at him, he was trying to control his laughter. What the hell is he laughing at? He doesn't exist for me either. Bleh! As I got up, our class teacher entered. He got lucky otherwise I would've thrashed him right there.

After hours, the day ended as usual and after the bell I went to library as promised to Aarya.

She was nowhere to be seen so I wandered across the sections to find something interestingly weird. I had a habit of reading that kind of stuff!

The ladder was there to reach the higher sections. In the hope of finding something, I climbed the ladder and surfed among the books. I found a book of unsolved mysteries but it was bit high. I tried reaching to it but whilst the struggle, some books fell on the other side.

I could hear the voice and a little cry of someone. I squinted my eyes and tried to rewind the time but nothing happened. I climbed down to see who was there then suddenly, a familiar and hateful voice fell into my ear.

"Are you dumb or stupid?" It was 27.

"Is there any difference between those?" It felt like he was hit by the books. I felt happy.

"It seems that you are stupid."

"Then why waste time talking to a stupid person? Go away Mr. Intelligent! "

"The books hit the back of my head." His voice was getting deep with every word. Other students gathered around.

"You can catch a paper ball but you cannot see books? And— it was unintentional."

"Apologize to me, right now!"

"I don't think my apology will reach you because I don't exist for you, so... goodbye!" I hit his shoulder with mine and crossed him.

Happiest moment of life! I argued to him and won. Total victory, Total savagery!

Aarya popped from the other side if the stack.

"Oh Sara, found you!" She made a little run.

I helped her solving questions. In half an hour, we were done.

"I am going to Vijay sir, you can go to the building."

"Okay then, see you!"

Slowly wandering and strolling, I reached to Vijay sir's cabin. He was inside and that was good otherwise it would be nearly impossible to find him! I knocked the door.

"Yes, come in!"

I was entering into the insulting fox's den.

"What happened?"

"I need permission to visit home."

"Your dadi is in city, right?"

"Yes sir."

"You could've gone on Sunday?"

Regular class was alright but he really didn't have to cross question here.

"That day, she was out of station." I couldn't tell him that we went to fun city that day and I also lost my memory of five minutes!

"Hmm...Only for a day and then you won't be able to for next six months." I know the rules!

"How's your project going?"

I blinked speedily. He should not be asking that question.

"It's in progress."

What are you doing in the project?"

"Um...I am reading about the topic."

"What is the topic?"

"Rusting." I remembered it vividly.

"Are you enjoying it?" He had hope in his eyes. He knew I hate his subject.

"I don't know." *What exciting things could happen while rusting some iron nails?*

"Then know about it." He finally signed.

"You have permission for today. Report back tomorrow till afternoon. "

I thanked him left. I rushed to the room and changed into trousers and jacket, packed a shoulder bag with a few things and went to Parul. I said goodbye to her and told her to say bye to boys from my side.

I walked to the nearby bus station. The bus was already there so I ran towards it and boarded it. The bus was full, there were no seats vacant so I had to travel by standing. The home was around fifteen kilometres away. After an hour, I reached the lane where my home was.

A sense of sadness was sinking inside.

I reached to the black iron door of my home but I lifted my head up and looked at the opposite end. Mahi's house was there but she was not. Some other people were living there but my eyes went to the roof. A sense of grieve came at surface but flown time suppressed it inside. I took a long deep breath.

"Dadi!" I shouted from the door.

My dadi, living her life in seventies came out. She was wearing green sari. Her face seem more wrinkled but her eyes still had the same shine. The government has provided a maid for her help. She takes care of her strict diet and that's why dadi is still capable of running marathon. I went to her and hugged her tightly.

"Oh, my Bittu is finally here!" She was overwhelmed. Bittu was the name she use to call me from my birth.

"Yes, your Bittu is here!" I was happy too.

"I missed you!" A wide smile popped.

"Now go and wash your legs! Today, your favourite masala dosa is in dinner."

"Really!"

"Yes! Now go!" I rushed to the bathroom.

After the clean-up, I went inside my room. The wave of nostalgia started eating me. My study table and my bed was there.

I drew the upper drawer. It had a photograph of Mahi and me in a frame. It was the first day of school. I was about to pick it up but dadi called me. I left the frame and marbles on the table.

"Yes dadi!" She was in the garden in the backyard.

"Pass me the basket, I have to put these." She was plucking fresh vegetables for sambhar.

I passed it to her and sat beside her.

"Bittu, how is school going?" The teacher inside her was coming outside.

She was a secondary school teacher back in time and dada was an army officer.

"Everything is great except for chemistry."

She laughed. "You still have that problem with yourself!"

"The thing is, I don't understand it and it doesn't fascinates me! After all, I am Mumma's daughter." She was also good in physics and good for nothing in chemistry.

"Hmm... how is everyone else?"

"Everyone is great. Prashant still teases Parul. Nikhil and Shree are good too and I got an enemy!" 27 flashed in my mind.

"Did you get a crush on someone?" I used to tell dadi everything.

"No, I am busy fighting against my enemy."

"Why?" Dadi stood up, I held the basket.

"Because, he is an obnoxious person."

"And how can you say that?"

"I have tons of verdicts to justify that he is an irritating person. I just fought with him two hours ago and it wasn't my mistake. Unintentionally, without my fault, the books fell by mistake." I narrated her the whole story.

"The reason for dropping those books was you, so it was your mistake. You should have said sorry. "

"If it was someone else, I would have said sorry...but before that incident, he told me that I don't exist for him. Whose blood will not be boiled? "

"That's right but I know you Bittu, you must've done something." I made a face.

"Dadi, I am your granddaughter, not him. Take my side not his!" We went to the kitchen.

"Okay, okay. Now bring me the mixer! "

I went to the cupboard and pulled the mixer out. She made the *imlie chutney*. I got little confuse, I don't take *imlie chutney* with dosa.

"For whom are you making this?"

"Ah! I forgot to tell you about this..." Suddenly a doorbell rang.

"I'll get the door!" I went outside.

I pulled the latch down and opened the door wide and then... ground under my feet vanished. *My smile dropped to the ground and got lost!*

Chapter-3

"You?" My eyes could not believe it.

"What are you doing here?" He seemed shocked but I had more right to be shocked.

"Me? You are standing at my house and you are asking what am I doing here? Wow!" I clapped.

"This is your house?" Distress was on his face too.

"Daaadiiii!" I shouted as loud as I could.

She came running.

"What happened?" She wiped her hands.

"Why is he here?" She looked at the door.

"Oh! Siddharth, come in. I guess you don't know him Bittu!"

"Really dadi?" That high class bastard gave me a look.

I know him more than you! No one cleared me yet, *what is he actually doing here? And why?*

"Dadi!!" She read the question mark on my face.

"I invited him to dinner." *What are the odds of that happening?*

"Why this charity? Why invite him to dinner?" My head was spinning.

"He lives two lanes away." She made him sit on the dining table.

"So?"

"Ohho...A week ago, I was coming from the market. A snatcher came and snatched my purse. This kind boy got my purse back so I invited him to dinner as a thanks." *Kind, my foot!*

"After that, he even walked me home. I came to know that he is in your school so I thought, I will invite him and coincidently you came today. Didn't you recognize him? Or is he in a different class? "

"He is in my class, unfortunately!"

"Bittu!" I knew what that for.

"Alright!"

"I need to prepare the dinner. You both talk!" Then she went away.

I crossed my hands. I hooked my brow up and then glared.

"What?" He was looking at me.

"Nothing, just seeing how much a person can be prideless! After knowing this is my house, you are still here."

"Are you serious? If I knew that this is your house and that sweet lady is your dadi, I would've never stepped at the door. "

"But now you know. So what's your plan? Get out!"

"I am here because of dadi, not because of you!"

"I am here because of dadi!" I imitated him.

I stepped into kitchen and dadi caught me making fun of him.

"Bittu! He is at our house for the first time. Be little hospitable." I guess she heard our conversation and— again I am at fault!

"Dadi!" That advice seemed impossible.

"We are in the same class, we are in the same section. He doesn't like me and neither do I. I cannot totally hate or can get along! I cannot avoid him but I can't patch up with him! "

"Bittu! I don't know, maybe outside!" She sighed.

"Go arrange the table. I'll call him for dinner." She went away.

Me and my words possess no value in this house!

I nodded and exhaled. Fine! He is at my home, I'll give him the begging of a delicious dinner and for the sake of dadi, I'll try not to fight.

I went to the kitchen to bring the plates and arranged the table for two. Dadi came inside with him.

Anger cooked again as his face came in front of me!

What is the need of dadi pampering and showing care to him this much? I came home after summer break and that for a short time, besides spending time with me, she is making him feel homely! Him? This high class bastard!

"Bittu!" Dadi's voice fell on my ears.

"Yes!" I turned my head to her.

"Sit down for dinner." That bastard was already sitting opposite me.

"Its okay dadi, I'll help you out with the chorus." I could not bear him in front of my eyes.

"It's rude! Sit down, Shalu will help me out." *God was playing with me again!*

Dadi served him sambhar in his bowl and served him imlie chutney. After that she went to the kitchen. I was looking at her that she didn't pour sambhar in my bowl!

I had to pour the sambhar by myself. The meter of anger was elevating. He got the special treatment, huh!

My eyes fell on him, he was looking somewhere else. I looked in the direction, he was looking at the house opposite to us. The house where Mahi used to live. Cold shivers ran through me, I squinted my eyes.

"Who lives there?" I opened my eyes.

"How would I know?"

"Are you sure that this is your house?" His hands were on the table. I exhaled.

"Last I knew, there was a nuclear family. It had three kids, a man and a lady. But why are you asking?" I rubbed my hands against each other. Cold shivers were not settling.

"No reason! It's been a while since I've been here. "

Meanwhile, Dadi brought us dosas. She served him first. *Does this family love me anymore?*

She served me after. *I have lost my value in my house!*

I started eating. As soon as I took the bite, it hit the spot. It's been very long since I've eaten dosas made by her hands. A sense of relief crept over. Soon dadi joined us for dinner. Shalu was making the rest of the dosas.

"So Siddharth, what do your parents do?" Dadi was sitting in the middle.

"Um... they both... martyred." I looked at him, I didn't expect that.

"Oh! Sorry. "

"It's okay! I was little back then. My uncle and aunt raised me. They both are fine. "

"Oh! So how are the dosas? "

"I've never tasted this much delicious food." Dadi smiled.

"Bittu! You want more? "

"Yes!" *Otherwise he will eat it all.*

"Siddharth, I'll get you one more." Dadi called for Shalu for dosas.

That bastard ate four dosas and I got filled up in two. He is not a human, he is an animal. Soon the dinner was over, dadi ate with me. My awaited moment was about to come. We will be saying goodbye to him!

He washed his hands and went to dadi to say goodbye, I couldn't hide my smile. Dadi sent him off to the outer door of the house. That bastard should've bought a gift for dadi, he doesn't have manners. He filled his bottomless stomach here and didn't bring a gift. Dadi was back after seeing him off.

"Dadi! Don't you think he should've bought a gift for you?"

"He is a boy and a kid. Boys don't understand those things and I was thanking him for his favour so there was no need."

"Dadi!" Bastard was back. I cried my invisible tears.

"I forgot this. I bought this for you!"

"Fake love, I am so sorry but its fake love!" I was humming.

It was a wooden case with a little metal latch on the side. Dadi opened it, it had a hairpin. A hairpin which had a peacock on the end.

"Did you like it?"

"It's beautiful! Thank you." They looked like long ago separated relatives.

"What about my gift? I am also at home, this is my house too!" My tongue was the only thing which couldn't be controlled.

"Bittu!" Dadi gave me a look.

"I'll give it to you in school." He falsely smiled.

I gave him a look. He is saying like he will give me one, high class bastard!

Soon he left, I had a sense of relief.

"Ohho!" Dadi was with me.

"What happened?" Plates were in my hand.

"He left his handkerchief. Bittu! Run after him and get him this." She pointed handkerchief at me.

"It's ok dadi, I'll return it to him in the school."

"No Bittu! It seems important. See there is a sword sign on it, it could be personal. He will be worried. "

"Dadi... I promise I'll return him in the school."

"Don't forget about it!" She gave me an ultimatum.

I gave her an innocent nod.

After cleaning up, I jumped on the bed and curled up on the sheet. Filled up stomach, tiredness made me sleep in no minute. I fell asleep thinking about him and his nonsense.

Birds were chirping, my eyes opened. I looked at the clock, it was ticking four. I sat up and rubbed my eyes. The sun was not up.

I inhaled a long breath and went to run in the layout. After two rounds, I started to run backwards. I was a little far from my home and was running and suddenly I bumped into someone. That someone was literal rock. I fell in front, my palms were little brazed.

"What the hell?" I stood up.

"Sorry...!" Familiar voice was there again.

I turned and encountered the brightest morning. It was him again. I thought he would be back to school after dinner but who knew he would brighten my morning like this. We stared at each other.

"Oh my god, it's you again!" I passed a taunt.

"Are you blind?"

"Well, I'd be not if my eyes were on my back and don't you have another question? Every time we meet, you always ask, are you dumb? Are you blind? Are you deaf? "

"I would be having an interesting question if you were an interesting person!" Then he went on running.

"Hey!" I ran behind him.

"You didn't even say sorry!" I caught him.

"I already did."

"At that time you didn't know it was me but as soon as you saw me, you switched your mode. You didn't even ask me if I was hurt! My hands... "

"Are you hurt?" This man always cut me in the middle. I clenched my fist.

He took my hand. My hands were brazed and blood was on the surface. He looked at me and pulled me and walked away.

"Hey! Where are you taking me? Leave... my hand!" His grip was tight and I couldn't compete with him that was for sure. He is an abnormal human, he doesn't know how humans interact. He stopped and turned and again I nearly bumped into him. The distance between us was close enough to hear each other's breath. I could hear his heartbeat next to my ear.

"Shut your mouth and walk with me!" He swallowed down his throat.

I couldn't say anything and walked behind him. My hand was still in his clutch. He turned to the corner and opened the main gate of a house.

It had a kind of modern architecture, my house had traditional architecture. Three stairs leading up to the small porch where the door opened to the carpet area. The energy around there was so positive, how come I never noticed such a refreshing area. The sun was up on the horizon.

He drew the keys from under the pot and unlocked the door. He pulled me in and took me straight to the basin. He opened the tap and put my palm under the running water.

"Really! You brought me here just because of this. "

"Can you shut yourself up for a while?"

"I haven't spoken a word from last two minutes."

"Then hold it for a minute more!

"All I asked was sorry! That's it..." He held my mouth.

"Bite your tongue, stupid!" He was again close to me and this closeness was burning me, I was not in a state of reacting anymore.

He turned the tap and pulled a towel and wiped the brazed area. He was putting so much pressure on the affected area that it started to hurt more.

"You know what, I don't need your sorry and it's a small wound. It won't kill me, so I take my leave now. See you in school!" I tried to get out. He pulled me back.

"Just stay where you are!" My hand was still in his hands.

He continued wiping, it was more painful than before. I was bearing it with my squinted eyes. He pulled a box from under the basin, first-aid box.

A bottle was there, he picked it. He poured some solution in cotton and applied it on the wound. It literally started burning and I could not control it.

"What the hell is that?" hot spice noises were coming out of my throat.

"It's a very effective solution. It will heal in no time."

"Less effective will work for me! I know… you did this on purpose. You just wanted to tease me, that's why you used such a strong solution. I named you right, you are really a high class bastard!" I went to the door.

"You named me a high class bastard?" He closed the door as I opened it. I turned my head.

"Is it wrong? Aren't you one? "

"It's quite right, chemistry topper!" He opened the door. He was smirking.

Burn! I gritted my teeth and went out stomping. Why the hell is he like that? Always overpowering me! Idiot! Argh! I ran to my house and went straight in shower.

I washed that solution out of my hand but it was still burning. What was the hell it is? *Bastard!*

I bathed and put on trousers. After jumping around like a monkey, I sat down on table for my brunch.

"Are you going to stay longer or are you going back to school?"

"I am going back! I didn't get permission to stay longer than a day and half. Don't worry dadi! I'll be here after six months. "

"If you won't come here then where will you go?"

"There is a facility to stay back at school!"

"You always want your word to be the last!" I smiled with my stuffed mouth. She stood up and went to the kitchen.

I finished my meal. Dadi was back with three containers.

"What is this?" I was in slight shock.

"This one has ladoos for Prashant and Parul, this one has aloo paratha for Shree and Nikhil and this one has moongfali patti for Siddharth. It's good for his health. "

"Dadi...what about my health? And you want me to give them everything? And I won't get anything?"

"There is a sufficient amount for everyone! Just scoop out for yourself from every container, ok! "

"I understand about others but why give to Siddharth?" I put the boxes in my bag.

"That boy is sweet and he doesn't have anyone to give him home food. His uncle and aunt aren't here! "

"Dadi but... wasn't the dinner enough?"

"Bittu! Don't argue and do as I say."

"Fine, I'll give it to him. Anything else ma'am?"

"No, now go, otherwise you'll miss your bus!"

"Oh right!" I face-palmed.

"Dadi!" I hugged her and touched her feet.

I went to the stop running with my bag. The bus was not there. The stop was not crowded but some people were there. Soon the bus arrived and I got in.

After half an hour, I was at the school. I thought that I might cross paths with Siddharth while coming but he wasn't there, good gracious!

It was about lunch time. I went to my room and changed into uniform and packed my school bag with boxes sent by dadi and my school bag. I scooped my part from all the containers.

My eyes searched for Vijay sir's cabin. I peeped from the glass piece on the door, he was not there.

"What are you looking at?" This voice belongs to the insulting fox.

"I came to report back."

"Fine, I'll sign the register."

Few minutes later, the recess bell rang. I met Aarya in the corridor.

"Oh! Sara, where you were? "

"I was at home."

"You know, something happened at school! I'll tell you later in class. "

"Ok, I'll catch you up later." She waved bye at me.

With box of paratha and ladoos and went to the dining area. My gang would be there and they were.

"Sara! Here!" It was Prashant.

I walked towards them. Their eyes had the lust of paratha. I handed them the box, and in minutes it was empty. My hands didn't had the smell of it!

"There was my paratha too!"

"You ate yesterday at home and we didn't, so I guess this is ok!" Shree clicked his tongue.

"Your dadi has magic in her hands. Sara! Where are my ladoos?"

"Here!" I sat on the chair.

Once, he said to dadi long ago that he like ladoos and from then whenever dadi can, she sends ladoos for him.

Everyone ate the ladoos and I was looking at.

"Heyy!"

"What?"

"I am hungry."

"There is the line, go get your plate." Parul wasn't in my reach otherwise I would've strangled her.

"Hey people! Has something happened at school?" I leaned on the table.

"Um... yes! We'll tell you later, eat first." Shree sounded serious.

"Hm..." I got my meal served.

"Guys! I am going out." Prashant pushed his chair.

"Probably going behind Shefali!" Parul shouted. Prashant leaned near her ear.

"You are right!" And then he went out.

"So, dadi is alright?" Nikhil relaxed in the chair.

"Yes, she is alright."

"How's your palms brazed? Did you fall somewhere?"

"Oh! I totally forgot to tell. You know what happened at home?"

"I am all ears."

"The most unexpected guest came home for dinner. Guess who?"

"Birthday clowns?"

"They are quite expected. That unexpected guest was Siddharth, can you imagine? This world is so small and still I never run into BTS!"

"How? Why did he come to your house?" Parul was grinning.

"Week ago, dadi went to the market for groceries. While coming to the house, her purse got snatched. Siddharth was the person who got dadi's purse back and then walked home with dadi. Dadi learned that he is in the same school as mine. She invited him for a thank you dinner and called him and coincidently, on the same date when I was supposed to go. Conclusively we had a little get-together last night." Nikhil laughed.

"Stop laughing! That animal ate four dosas. "

"And you fought with him over a dosa and that's why your hands are brazed?"

"No! This morning, I went for a run. Siddharth also lives in that layout. I bumped into him and fell and that's why I got this!" I pointed at my hand.

"You know! I don't have any words, I mean what should I say?" Nikhil was sill laughing.

"Don't say anything!" I stuffed my mouth with rice.

"My dadi likes that boy so much that she sent a box of moongfali patties for him!"

"Really? Can I get some?" Parul liked every food item in the world.

"Take some from my share! But... Have you seen him? I need to give it to him otherwise dadi will forget that I am her *poti*." I struggled with the last grain of rice in the plate.

"Nope!"

I went to the sink to put the plate down and traced back to the table.

"Let's go out!" We stood up and left.

"So, what did you guys do without me?" And then I hit Nikhil at the back. He groaned in pain.

"I am sorry! Are you hurt?" My eyebrows frowned.

"Yea!" He was trying to bear the pain.

"Is it aching?"

"Yea but don't worry, I'll be fine." He sat down.

"Should we go to infirmary?"

"No, little rest and I will be fine." The pain was clear on his face. I sat beside him.

"Why on earth you worked yourself out?"

"Um...I had my reasons."

"You know what Nikhil, we've been friends for the last six years and I still can't figure you out. You always have your situations and your reasons, you never tell me anything!"

This has happened a lot of times. I generally find him severely injured or missing for a while and whenever I ask him what happened. His forever response is, 'I had my reasons!'

"Sara...my situation and my reasons are the things which I don't share." We had this conservation before.

"Fine! Don't do drama. "

"See, that's why you are my best friend!" He landed his face on my shoulder.

We all spent our time in garden till the bell rang. I offered my hand to Nikhil.

"Let's go, I will walk to your class."

"For sure!" He took my hand in a girly way.

I left him at his class and then I went back to my class. The class was a little occupied by students. I looked at his seat, there was no bag under the desk. He is still not here.

"Boo!" It was Arya. I already sensed her.

"Ha! I am scared and dead."

"You never get scared!"

"I know!"

"So, how was your visit?"

"Nice!"

"You know something happened at school. Karan from the other section and some junior students are missing! "

"What?" My brain stopped working.

"Yea. Rumours are flying in the room. Some say that they are dead, some say that they probably snuck out! I don't know. "

"What?" I nearly screamed out.

"Shush! It's just a talk. I don't know if it's right or not but... students are quite terrified. Remember the girl's accident, then that happened and now students are missing!" I was just listening to her.

"I've heard news from the town too! People are getting killed and going missing. My instincts say something is not right."

Arya was the girl who believed her instincts more than any fact. I've seen this thing so many times that even I don't doubt her instincts.

"I just hope everything is fine and my instincts are wrong." The class bell rang.

We exchanged glances and went to our seats. My eyes rolled over his table. A mixed emotion was on the surface, didn't know what it was.

The class commenced with the lessons and I lost myself in the story. The day passed and school ended. We all walked to our buildings.

"How's your injury now?" We climbed down the stairs.

"It's fine." Nikhil moved his shoulder.

"It's been a while I haven't seen him!" Parul started ranting.

"Boo!" Prashant scared Parul from behind, Shree was behind him. He pulled him back.

"I am sick of this potato head!" The battle started.

"Oh! A girl with no brain cell is talking. "

"You are saying like you got tons of them! You… Shefali chaser!"

"You Siddharth liker!"

"Enough!" Shree screamed in between.

We were near the oak tree. Nikhil and I exchanged glances. We smiled and understood the situation, actually Shree's reaction was funnier. We walked towards the building while talking about the day and soon we reached there.

"See you in the evening! Be ready on time. "

"For what?"

"Oh! I think I forgot to tell you. Yesterday, a notice was circulated. As we are in senior year, every evening, we have to be present at evening routine. "

"Is that compulsory?"

"Of course! It is the same as the morning routine but with a different pair of exercises. Reporting time is half past five. "

"Okay then let me rest till then." I slammed my door and jumped in bed.

After cleaning myself up, I looked at my desk. The books in front of me were yelling at me to open them. I had to study for the final selection in the university after the completion of senior year.

I drew a heavy book named 'Chemistry for Everyone'. I can challenge this title totally, it's not for everyone. Believe me! No one knows this more than me.

I opened the book and went to the topic of nomenclature. After five minutes, I found myself blinking my eyes very slowly. My body was falling into the black hole of sleep. Slowly, darkness crept before my eyes.

My eyes opened with a jerk. Drool was sticking to my chin and to the pages of the book. My face was red because of the edges of the book. The book left its impression on me.

I slapped myself on both the cheeks and buried myself into the book. I didn't understand enough but I learnt the rules. Logical part was never a problem. Soon, the clock ticked five. The reporting time was half past five.

I stood up and stretched myself and went to the bathroom. The tracksuit was hanging on the hanger and waiting for me to wear it. Parul barged inside.

"You ready?" Parul was still at the door.

My eyes rolled at the clock, it was quarter past five. "Give me a second." I quickly tied my hair.

"Done!" We went out of the room and ran straight to the ground.

"Formation pattern?" I was still running.

"Same as always!" She meant the morning pattern.

Cadets were already there and that PE teacher with his trainer was also there. We were on time and the roll call started.

A familiar voice fell into my ears. It was him. He was standing there in his black tracksuit. His hair was stuck up and were fighting to fall down. He caught me looking at him. His eyes caught my eyes. A sensation was running through me, what was it? No idea! He slightly snapped his fingers, it broke my lostness. I looked in front, it would've been the problem if the PE caught me.

Why the hell was I looking at him? Did I zone out? I never spare a chance for him to insult me. I don't know what he will think of me. Wait! He won't think anything. I don't exist for him!

Soon the routine started. As it was the first day, we were wearing off. After the routine, we all were sat down to rest a bit. My eyes roamed around.

Parul looked dead exhausted, Prashant looked fine. 27 looked fine too but his hair won the fight and was on his forehead.

A whistle blew signalling the sports match! Our squadron was up for volleyball match. Other two went for basketball.

Eight random calls of cadets decided the team. There were two courts so everyone got on team. Parul was in other team, facing Prashant while I was on different court with the role of setter.

The game started with the whistle. We all knew how to play so the match was competitive. Everyone was shouting for the serve and receive.

In the end, we lost the game by one score because of the rear court spike.

Second match was called and this time bastard was on the team. As the match went on, that guy made everyone drop their jaw. He became the star quickly.

His game was actually good! He saved the ball several times and remained in the spotlight for the whole match.

After the end of the match, he was surrounded by the squadron cadets. They were patting his back and giving him compliments. Some girls screamed their throats out for him. He was smiling, probably enjoying the girly screams of his names. He instantly became the crush of so many girls. I looked at him, he caught my glance for a second.

"Non-existent high class bastard!" I mumbled and went to Nikhil.

The basketball matches wrapped up too. After a minute, the whistle blew. Everyone stood back to their places and after that, we were dispersed. We all joined each other for the walk till the buildings.

"Well played setter!" Nikhil squeezed my shoulders.

"I know!" I acted cool.

"... But Siddharth totally blew everyone away. He is perfect for playing volleyball. His spikes were on different levels." Prashant jumped in between.

"Yes! His spikes were so perfect. I want to learn from him, probably I'll make him my friend!"

"Don't you dare!" It was Parul.

"Don't you go near him! You'll infect him with your dumbness. "

"You cannot underestimate Prashant in volleyball!" I was listening to them.

"See, sensible people know things, unlike you! ... Sara, I must say, you have improved in tossing." Parul clenched her fist in the air. I grinned.

We all reached the building. We parted from the boys and climbed the stairs.

"The image of him playing at the court is still in front of my eyes." Parul smiled.

"I gotta admit, he is good at this!" I sighed.

"Of what? Being on mind?" She giggled.

"I... I meant volleyball!" I subconsciously stuttered.

She came close to my face and squinted her eyes.

"Good to hear! That you finally started admitting nice things about him." She changed her expressions very quickly.

"Oh hello! It's sportsmanship. If your opponent is good at something, you must appreciate it and I still hate him as a human." I disgusted.

"Alright, Miss setter." We reached our rooms.

"See you at dinner." She exhaled, she seemed tired.

I kicked my shoes and fell on the bed.

I hate that guy.

Suddenly my eyes fell on the box of moongfali patties. I had to give it to him, should I go right now? It will be not good if I gave this in school or will it be?

Argh! Coin!

I pulled the drawer out and pulled a coin. If head, then yes otherwise no. I flipped the coin high and caught it in the middle. I closed my one eye and peeped from the corner of the other eye. God likes to play pranks, it was heads!

I will give this box to him and then I won't be bothered and plus if I gave this in school, it would not be nice. Even if he says something savage then it won't be in front of anyone. I nodded my head in yes and wore shoes again and climbed down.

The box was in my hand and ran to the boys' building. I reached the ground floor counter. I didn't know his room number or anything. There was a guy standing near the notice board. He was definitely not in my batch, which concludes that he is junior to me. I walked to him.

"Listen!" He turned.

"Yes... good evening senior!" I was right.

"Do you know Siddharth? He is your senior. "

"Yes, I do know him. He is a good friend of cadet Nikhil." Nikhil was a popular guy in whole school.

"Okay then! Do me a favour, call him downstairs. "

"Okay." Then he ran upstairs.

I never step into the boy's building. You never know in which condition they would be roaming. I remember once going inside for urgent call and ended up witnessing a guy in his underwear.

I was out of the building and stood near the short cement boundary. That boy's words wonderstruck me, he is a good friend of Nikhil! I never saw them talking in the school or anywhere. Siddharth is in my class, when did they get time to bond?

"What happened?" He was here. I turned.

"Why'd you call me?" He caused me distress as soon as he opened his mouth.

"Oh... I just wanted to see the apple of my eye!" I got dramatic.

"If you wanna talk crap then I am leaving!"

"You are the one who provoked me!"

"Come to the point." He crossed his arms. I stretched the box in front of him.

"Dadi sent this for you. Take this and don't waste a crumb of it and here... your handkerchief. "

"Say thanks to dadi."

"Okay, I'm leaving." I turned and was about to walk.
"Wait!"

"What?" I turned. "Do you want me to compliment your game?" My tongue could never be controlled.

"No!" He chuckled.

"How's your bruise from this morning?" I looked at my palm.

"They are alright and they were not serious." I gritted my teeth. I remembered how pissed I was at him.

"Hm..." He tapped his fingers on the box.

"Um...thank you for returning the handkerchief. It was my father's." I sensed his sincerity but I didn't want to admit it.

"Alright...Can I leave now, if I have your permission?"

"Wait! One more thing, stay here." He ran upstairs in his building.

After a minute he appeared from the gate with a notebook. He walked towards me.

"Here." He stretched the notebook before me.

"What is this?"

"Chemistry notes on rusting. This will help you in learning about the project. "

"I don't know, should I take this as a favour or an insult?" My face squared.

"Take this as a favour because I am giving this to a non-existing person." And then he left.

I could sense the smirk on his face from behind.

An insulting smirk!

"Giving him this time was the best decision ever!" I mumbled and nodded.

I walked back to my building and threw the notebook on the table. I fell on the bed again and closed my eyes. My heart was beating too fast, it was because of the running and climbing stairs. I got up and changed my clothes. Today was the first day of the evening routine, it was tiring but it was fun too.

I went to the table and flipped some pages from the notebook he gave me. His handwriting was somewhat different and beautiful. The words in ink on the paper were perfectly placed. I looked at my notebook which was lying beside. The words were fighting to get closer to each other and they all were much slanted to the right. My face made up. *Whatever! Having nice handwriting doesn't makes him a good person!*

I read through some points, they were neatly written and were quite easy to understand. I've never read this much clear and precise explanation of any chemistry topic.

That definition surprised me because I understood it very well with the logic behind it. I was impressed by his skill but of course I will never admit this in front of him.

"Hooooooo!" Parul barged in. She leaned on the door.

"What?" I put the notebook on the table.

"I...am...hungry!" She tried to deepen her voice. She was dramatic.

"Me too!"

We hurriedly walked down the stairs and went to the dining hall. I was behind her. We entered the hall and it was a bit unexpected. Almost everyone was there at this much early time. At this time, generally the hall is nearly empty but today it is completely full. I guess everyone was hungry from today's evening routine. We grabbed our plates and lined up. Regular meal was there but it seemed like a fancy dinner to everyone. All were hungry from their soul's stomach.

We looked for an empty spot. While looking, we found the boys there too. We went to them and adjusted seats among them.

They all were eating like this was their last meal of life and no one was talking to anyone. Everyone hurriedly finished the super and went outside.

"Finally, I am feeling heaven!" Prashant was a different pack of drama.

"Seriously, I was so hungry that if I didn't eat that bite at that moment, I would've died of hunger."

"Then we would be able to eat more." Prashant and Parul started again.

"Can't you guys stop fighting for a moment?" Shree interrupted.

"No they can't. That's the fuel to their soul." I turned and started to walk backwards.

"You know guys, leave them! You guys...keep going, we are all ears." Nikhil pulled both of us behind.

They agreed to Nikhil's advice and went on.

"Look at your choice, Shree!" Nikhil whispered.

"I know, one of the reason why I like her."

"Oh well well!" We chuckled and went ahead.

Everyone was out in the campus. I saw Siddharth at a bench. Things clicked my mind.

"Nikhil! Tell me one thing honestly. "

"You know when you quote this, I just want to lie. Have I ever lied? Maybe I have...what is it?" He chuckled.

"Are you good friends with Siddharth?"

"Umm... yes! We are, kind of. "

"When did you boys grow your bond?"

"He lives opposite to my room. It's natural and— why are you asking this? "

"I didn't expect that you guys are good friends. I never saw you guys talking. "

"Yeah... because we didn't, without any reason!" He pinched his chin.

"Well why didn't you tell me?"

"You hate that guy and you both keep running away from each other. That's why I preferred not to rub salt on your wounds." I looked at him, he was trying to tease me.

"So how much of the stuff you guys tell each other?"

"We do tell each other some stuff, not deep. Yea... he talked about you once when you were about to go home for a day. Sometimes he gets really irritated by you but he doesn't resent you. He is a good and genuine guy."

"Really!" I was quite shocked.

After the amount of fight and hate we exchanged, I thought cussing each other is the only thing we could do about each other.

"Yeah! But you... my friend, resent him a lot. "

"It's... his choice! I'll play according to my choice. "

"I am feeling kind of sleepy!" Shree yawned and stretched his hands.

"It's getting late too, we have a morning routine too. Let's go!" Nikhil said to everyone.

We started walking towards our buildings. While returning, I saw him sitting on the bench and rolled my eyes away. He is one acting bastard!

Parul and I climbed stairs to our rooms.

"See you tomorrow." She was yawning too.

"Okay, bye." I opened my door and went inside and went straight to bed.

Chapter-4

Next morning, the alarm rang. I woke up on time for the morning routine.

As we went down, we heard some girls whispering something to each other. I couldn't understand but concluded that some rumour must be there.

As we reached the ground floor, intense tension was floating. All the care-takes were talking in group. I hit my elbow on Parul.

"Do you know anything?"

"How am I supposed to know anything? I just came down— and yesterday, I slept like a log." We were still walking towards the ground.

We reached the ground. Cadets were all lined up.

Everyone there had a weird kind of expression. No was talking but their eyes were screaming.

While the routine, I spotted a scar on Siddharth's neck. It was on the back side. It was weird and it was weirder for me to notice it.

Soon after the end of routine, we were attending the classes. I spotted Aarya sitting on the seat behind. First bell didn't rang yet.

"Hey! Aarya, has something happened? Everyone seem tensed!"

"Oh! Last night, a boy from boy's building was found behind our building. That boy was with a huge cavity in his torso. His blood was everywhere. This morning when I was at my window, I found him dead." She was talking low.

"What the hell?" I was completely dazed.

"That was a terrible thing that has happened till now! But you know what...I expected that kind of thing. After the girl who got killed, those boys who went missing and the news from the town, anyone can expect it. "

"What'd you mean?"

"Don't you see an invisible connecting string between these incidents?"

"What kind of string?"

"My gut says that all these murders and accidents are connected in some way."

"Really?"

"Yea, but it is just a feeling."

The bell rang. Soon the insulting fox entered with notes of chemistry in his hands. The class was going on with the non-understandable lesson of insulting fox. Unknowingly, I thinking about what Aarya said.

The lunch bell rang and I stretched myself. I needed a damn break with all those thoughts running through my mind.

Maybe if I talk to Nikhil, I will feel a bit light. Nikhil was already standing there as I went outside. We walked downstairs towards the dining hall. As we were walking, everything seemed normal. I guess some students don't have any idea about the incident!

Only God knows after what this school authority is? They hid each and every mishap from students and kept us in the dark. There is no safety net for students in the campus, I have seen nothing. Regular schedule is being followed even after accidents.

We reached the dining hall, everyone was already there with their plates. We stood in line for the meal. After some time we took our filled plates and sat on a table.

"Do you guys know about the accident?" Parul took her bite.

"Yes! He was one year junior to us."

"Some students don't know about it yet. What you think, will they tell us?"

"No chance! I've heard them. They don't want students to panic." Prashant answered.

"They might have their reasons. What if juniors came to know about it? Students will probably run away from here!"

"The man gotta point." Prashant joined Nikhil.

"But they should tell everyone. Everyone should be alerted by this. Everyone will step carefully. It's a life and death game, everyone has to be safe!" Parul seemed concerned.

"Parul! Cool down." Shree took her.

"I... I am just...it's not justice to the people who lose life without any reason. "

I could understand Parul's words. She had a past too.

When she was little, her family went on a day trip. They halted for a while as she was being cranky about something so her father took her to a snack shop and parked the car on the roadside. When they returned, they found the car crashed into a small construction and everyone, her twin sisters and her mother were all covered in blood. They rushed to the hospital but they were declared dead. After some time, his father had to go to his service and she had no one to look after. Her father left her in the shelter of his older sister. Her father's older sister raised her. His father rarely met her after that.

As she said those words, we all looked at each other. She just scratched her unhealed wound of heart unintentionally.

"Parul! Please, cool off!" Shree took her hand.

"I am fine!" Parul stared at her plate.

"We gotta be strong. We all will be in the armed forces and won't know on which bullet our name is written. That is the path we chose! Now eat!" Prashant made a little speech.

We were stunned by his little speech. The boy was speaking facts. None of us answered him back and ate our lunch in silence.

As the lunch finished, we all went to the oak tree. As we were walking around, someone called for Prashant so he left us there. Shree was calming Parul down. Nikhil and I were strolling around so I decided to bring up the things which I wanted to discuss.

"Nikhil, do you hear the daily news from the town?"

"Yeah, things are happening."

"Do you know Aarya, from my class?"

"Yes, she is in my squadron."

"Oh! Umm... She thinks that the incidents in town and incidents that occurred in our school are interrelated. "

"Why... why? Why does she think that?"

"It's her gut feeling."

"See, there is a possibility that these things are related but there is a possibility that it's not. It could be a coincidence and it's impossible for any intruder to come here."

"I understand your point but..."

"Don't overthink. There are some strings and dots which are not revealed. You cannot conclude anything."

"I guess you are right."

"You know because of this thing, I was distracted the whole time and Vijay sir caught me. I remembered something from Siddharth's notes so I made an excuse and saved myself otherwise... "

"Siddharth's notes?"

"Yeah..!" The bell rang, the lunch was over.

"The lunch is over. Let's go!"

I went to the class and sat at my table. The literature class was about to start so I pulled the textbook.

"Sara!" I heard my name.

I lifted my head up and looked at the person. This heavy voice was familiar but I've never heard my name in it. I saw him, it was Siddharth. He was looking at me, straight into my eyes. His hair was on his forehead as ever and the cuff of the blazer were collected at his elbow. My mind started running, why did he call me? Have I done something? Is he about to insult me?

"Yes!" My mind and eyes coordinated.

"Have you read the notebook which I gave you?"

"Nooope!"

"Do it already. We need to prepare for the project. It will help in proceeding further in project."

I scoffed. What is he trying to show here? I mimicked him

"It will help in proceeding further in project."

He caught me mimicking him. He looked with his frowned brows.

I quickly shifted my gaze and hid my face with squinted eyes. After gathering a bit of courage, I turned my head and opened an eye. He was grinning. What kind of stupid and abnormal person he is? Why the hell is he grinning? Bastard! My eyes were on him and then again he caught me looking at him. He stopped grinning and I turned my face. He really is abnormal!

Soon the teacher came and the class started. After tiring classes for four hours, the school went off. We all were ready to head back.

"So... commander! Tomorrow is your birthday. "

Oh yeah right! Tomorrow is my birthday. I did forgot about it, shit! Hectic schedule and other distracting things like accidents in school and that bastard totally engaged my brain. I totally forgot that I am gonna be seventeen tomorrow!

"Your expression says that you forgot about it." Nikhil caught me.

"Um... yeah! Kind of, I did. You know, birthdays were never fascinating to me."

"Yeah I know and I know the reason too."

"What do you think?"

"Will my parents make it?"

"I don't know but —you still have us and your dadi. Your dadi will definitely come."

"... But I really want to see Mumma and Papa. It's been a while. Mumma said that she will come."

"Just have hope. Well... do you need anything for your birthday?"

"What will you get me?"

"Anything!"

"Then... give me a promise that you will never leave my side! ...I know this dramatic but I am afraid after hearing 'incidents'." I stretched my palm before him.

He held his palm against mine. "I promise Sara, I will be by your side until my last breath."

"I didn't mention last breath."

"It was from my side." He smiled.

Everyone was talking and running behind, soon we were at our buildings.

"I am tired." As Parul said this she leaned on her door and locked it.

I was still standing there with a pouted mouth.

"Okay!" My room welcomed me.

I changed clothes and picked up his notebook and read it. The monthly test can be announced any time. I studied for an hour and this was the first time I was able to understand chemistry this much in such a short time. My body was reaching its limit. I was again in the lightless pit of sleep!

The alarm rang and my eyes opened. I was really exhausted so I slept like a log but woken by the alarm. The routine was about to start so I changed into the tracksuit quickly.

Parul came on her usual time and then we went to the ground. The routine started, this time while exercise, I saw Siddharth's neck mark again. The mark looked like a cracker burst. I didn't give it much thought and ignored it.

This time I was up for basketball match with Siddharth. He was excellent in basketball too. He was this excellent that he took every pass which I was supposed to take! Bastard!

He was again in spotlight and was the star of the evening. As the match ended up, cheers of last evening repeated!

"Did you see my match?" Parul came running to me.

"Yeah, I saw it. Did you see mine?"

"Yea..." She reached a different level. "Siddharth was so cool on the court. I didn't expect him to be this good in basketball. His shooting skills and running... woah!"

"Yea... I am so happy that you saw me." My taunt and irritation was clear.

"Come on, you know he is good then... "

"Will you please stop talking about him? I am so pissed right now that if he comes in front of me then he will lose his head!"

"Who will lose his head?" Prashant heard it with a water bottle in his hand.

"Mr. Siddharth!" My teeth were rubbing against each other.

"Oh that guy! Yea he should lose his head for your sake but— he is good at games. I told you, I should go and shake his hand for friendship." He wiped his sweat.

"Do you wanna die?" I gave him a look.

"Okay tell me, what bad has he done to you?"

"He stole the ball from me at the game. I was just running here and there. I was the shooting guard and so was he, so the responsibility gets split, not taken! I was feeling nothing at the court like why the hell was I even standing there? They would've won if I wasn't there! "

"Sara!"

"What?" Prashant rolled his eyes to point behind me.

I looked back, Siddharth was standing there. Stunned! I could only conclude that from his face. It felt like it him hit hard, did my words hurt him? Wait! Will he get hurt by a non-existent person?

I did nothing and kept staring. He looked at me and then at Prashant and Parul. I swallowed my saliva down the throat. Anger and frustration seemed melting in my eyes.

He put his bottle down and went with a lowered head.

What is up with his guy? Here I was distressed about the whole game and he didn't blurt a word? He heard everything, I guess and he didn't react? He is really a high class bastard!

"Leave! It's ok." Prashant tapped my shoulder.

"Did he listen to everything?" Parul expressed my curiosity.

"Ah...Sara, tomorrow is your birthday!" Prashant tried to change the atmosphere.

"Yes... Sara is gonna be a grown up." Parul clapped her hands.

I turned to her and raised my one brow. "Do you think birthdays fascinate me?"

"Why not? It's your birthday, you are going to be seventeen and..." The whistle blew.

We gathered back in the formation and then dispersed. Nikhil and Shree joined us on the way back.

"Sara is going to be seventeen tomorrow? Right?" Shree hooked his hand on my neck.

"Yes!"

"Such a grown up! Be a good kid after such an age. Respect elders and your friends. Don't be a tomboy every time and talk nicely." He sighed.

I hit him in his stomach with the elbow. "Yes dadaji!" I taunted.

"So Sara... is there any wish you have for your seventeenth birthday?"

"Nah... not really. My birthdays are just like a normal other day, it really doesn't affect me much except for giving me false hope that my parents will visit me, together!"

"Just be hopeful, maybe something miraculous could happen at your birthday." We reached the building.

"Okay people, let's meet up at dinner." Prashant waved his hand.

We all headed back to their rooms. Parul was climbing stairs with me.

"Sara... what is your deal with Siddharth?"

"What do you mean? And that is so sudden and irrelevant right now! "

"No, I am just asking. You two are in the same class so do you guys talk a lot?"

"A lot? Yeah, we fight a lot, if that counts as talking."

"No, seriously Sara! I have looked at him, there is a different vibe between you too."

"What bullshit are you talking about, Parul?"

"No, it's a feeling. I am just saying. There are so many strings between you and him."

"Parul! Shut the hell up. There is nothing." We were in front of our rooms.

"I am just saying."

"But why?"

"No reason!" She turned to her door and went in.

What the hell just happened? Why the hell Parul is saying all this? She has gone crazy! I turned to my door and swung it open and went inside.

Soon the dinner time ticked in the clock. I went over to Parul's room.

"Hey! I am hungry. Let's go." She flipped the notebook on the table and locked the room.

We went downstairs, the boys weren't there so we stood in line for dinner. We went to a table and started to eat, soon the boys came and joined us.

"I so wanted to celebrate your birthday at 12 o'clock!" Parul clapped her hands.

"Yea! Celebrating birthdays at midnight is a different level of thrill." Shree took his bite.

"What if we do that?" Prashant's brain started working.

"And what will you do?" Nikhil questioned.

"It takes the risk of climbing the roof!" Prashant's eyes gleamed.

"Roof is closed... totally sealed." Parul rubbed her palms.

"What about the mountain where we climb every day?" Parul suggested.

"Good idea." Prashant shook hands with her.

"Um... no! The mountain at night is not safe." Nikhil condemned the idea.

"Why?" Parul wiped her mouth.

"Did you forget about the incidents which happened in the past few days? And it is impossible to go there. There are no lights up there."

"Enough!" I banged my hands on the table.

"No need to experience any kind of thrill or adventure. We will cut the cake in broad daylight, that's it."

"Huh...then we will only get to celebrate the birthday at night in university." Prashant faked his distress.

"Alright, no more drama." Nikhil finished his meal and got up.

"Here take my plate too!" Shree finished his meal too.

"Mine too!" Parul pushed her plate.

"Wait! Here." Prashant gave his plate too.

"I have no reason of not giving you my plate!" I put the plate above on the stack.

He looked at us and exhaled. He nodded his head and took the plates out to the sink area. We all got up and washed our hands and went to the oak tree.

"Today is the last night you will feel like you are sixteen." Shree commented.

"So you are saying that from tomorrow, I'll suddenly feel old?"

"Umm... yes because you would've ended your sweet sixteen era."

"Nikhil, make his mouth shut. He is talking nonsense."
He was beside me.

"Shree! That was such a lame taunt." Prashant hooked
onto his neck.

"If you wanna say something then say... from
tomorrow, she will be a mature girl and won't fight with
Siddharth!" I hit him.

"That was lame too!" Nikhil said.

"It's going to be her birthday, don't ruin it." Parul
talked as a supportive friend.

"Everyone!" I jumped in front. "Don't exaggerate, it's
just a normal day when dadi will come and we will cut a
cake. That's it and now no more discussion!" I turned and
walked.

"Fine! No one will talk about it." Parul took my hand.

We all strolled for a while and then walked back to our
buildings and greeted the night.

"Happy birthday in advance!" Shree screamed from
the gate.

"Happy birthday!" Nikhil and Prashant were in unison.

"Okay, thanks! Good night." I waved back.

"My stomach is aching so I am going to sleep and
happy birthday!" Parul opened her door.

"It's alright! And if you can't, don't bother yourself to
awake at midnight." She was not alright.

"I love you!" She gave me a flying kiss. Her face was a
little pale.

I went inside and sat in the chair. I drew the notebook
and the book and started to study. I leaned back on the
chair and put my hands in the pocket. Wait! What is it? It
was a piece of paper. What is it? I unfolded it.

*I didn't mean to steal the ball from you and we wouldn't
have won without you. You were needed at the court. I am*

sorry if I hurt you!
~Siddharth

Has he drunk? That person is saying sorry to me! Wow, my birthday had the best welcome like this... and from where this landed into my pocket? I didn't see him after the match! Did anyone else...Nikhil! Huh... why does he have to side with that guy? And what am I supposed to do now... with this? Should I go say that I am honoured to read sorry from you? He is really a bastard species. I resumed my study and tossed the note into the dustbin.

The time passed and lights outside switched dim. The gates are closed now. I was a little tired and had to wake up early tomorrow with the enthusiasm as it is going to be my birthday, so I went to sleep and shut the lights out except my lamp.

Will they come? Or only Mumma will come? What if only dadi came? I was changing sides of the bed. I couldn't sleep, my eyes had an urge to sleep but my mind won't shut them. I took the torch and clicked its light on and off while my mind hovered over the hope of seeing my parents together.

The lights outside were totally dim and the air was blowing nice. I sat up, my mind was messed up. I slid the window up for some fresh air and lingered over the window sill. The air was nice so I leaned my head on the window gate.

Suddenly something jumped in front of my window. The light was dim but I could figure out the shadow. My eyes were enlarged, collecting every ounce of fear. I held my breath. What is it? It looked like a person. The head was covered in some sort of cloth and a sword was hanging from the waist. That thing crouched on the pillar of the shade of the entrance. My heart throbbed and my legs shook. What is that? The torch was still in my hands. Past days incidents were clicking in my mind. The lamp in my room was still lit.

"Who is there?" I flashed the torch at that thing with a stutter in voice and shake in hands.

I would have been a donkey in my previous birth! If this shadow turns out to be killer, then I am going to be tomorrow's headline.

A girl died before completing her sweet sixteen era!

Suddenly, it looked straight at me. That thing ripped me with its sudden gaze at me. It was surely a human but... was it human? The sweat was all over my face and my soul was ready to leave my body. The torch was in my hands. I tried to close the window but damn that latch. I was panicking and with another blink, that thing jumped over me and pushed me down from the bed.

My soul has already left the body but my survival instincts were working.

I hit the floor and the torch rolled away. It was a human and a male figure. I could feel the masculine weight. It pushed me further by the shoulders and covered my mouth but I had an army person's blood in my veins. All the learning was striking inside the brain.

I joined my hands, making a fist and with a swoop, I hit his both hands. He fell over me and with the moment, I was over him and clutched his neck with my arm. I wanted to scream but my throat was already choked.

I tried to uncover his face but he pressed his mask against his face. He was surely a normal human. He wasn't attacking me but defending himself and I was in total attacking mode to save my ass.

With the struggle, I managed to take off his black hood and then I saw something. The ground beneath my feet vanished like it was never there.

It was the bursting cracker mark on the neck.

I froze for a moment while he threw me to the other side.

Was it Siddharth?

"Siddharth!"

Chapter-5

My brain stopped working as I saw that mark. With that surprise, his name got out of my mouth subconsciously. He froze for a moment and looked at me.

The same coldness which I've seen before! He blinked and looked at the window. He was about to leave.

"Show me your face!" I climbed his back.

"Show... me... your... face!" I was not backing down.

I wanted confirmation if I guessed him right. There was a possibility that this could be some other person and— this person could kill me if he crossed his patience line.

I was still on his back, trying to unmask him from behind. He tried to unlock my hands from his neck but I had a different determination. I needed to know if it was him, why is he dressed like some ninja? And what is he really doing? Or did I catch some notorious person?

I was so focused on taking his mask off that I didn't see his move coming. I felt a sudden pull from behind and got thrown away. I tried to get hold of myself and grabbed whatever I could and fell on the floor, again.

Thud! I heard a voice. I opened my eyes and my breath stopped. He was over me and his mask which he was wearing was now in my hands.

It was really him. The lamp had enough light to make his face recognizable. He looked at me, he was balancing himself on his arms. My heart throbbed, it's really him.

Siddharth, the guy with whom I fought, is a kind of guy who wears ninja clothes and roams with a sword at night.

It was all silent, only my breaths could be heard. I could hear my own heartbeat from inside. My heart was about come out of my throat.

His face made up as his crime got caught. He snatched the mask cloth out of my hand and stood up. I stood up too, he tied up his mask again and covered his head in a hood.

"What... "

"Shut up and forget about this till next tomorrow." He put his fingers in between my eyebrows.

As he said this, something happened inside. I wanted to ask things but couldn't. My eyes closed and then everything faded into nothing.

I heard my name, in a faded voice.

A jerk on my shoulders and a hard slap.

"Get up you donkey!" It was Parul. My eyes opened.

"Get ready quickly, sleepy log!" She was gritting her teeth.

"Why? What is the time?" I looked at the clock.

Damn! It was six. It's time to report on the ground. My head was spinning, I was not in my senses.

"Did you get drunk last night?"

"No, my head is heavy!"

"Get up and get ready otherwise you will be scolded by the PE on your birthday. I am waiting for you."

"You know what? You go report to the ground, I will come."

"You sure? Don't sleep again. "

"Hm... I won't."

"Be quick then!" She left the room with the spare key of my room.

What happened last night? Why is my head spinning? I tried to remember, a sudden strike of thought. Siddharth! My eyes opened, everything was flashing in front of my eyes. Was that a dream? How he came in and his mark and his mask!

I looked at the window, it was closed but the torch was still lit under the table. It was not a dream but how did I fall asleep? I squinted my eyes, then remembered him putting his finger between my brows. He must've done something but why? I exhaled, it's really not time to think.

I rushed into the bathroom and changed into the track suit and ran to the ground.

As I reached there, the squadron was doing exercise. I went there in the middle of it.

"Cadet!" I heard PE. *Get ready for your birthday, Sara!*

"Yes sir!"

"Why are you late? State your reason!"

What was I supposed to say? Dear PE, last night a boy broke into my room and none other than that 27 in the squadron and he is not a normal person. Please excuse me!

"I overslept, sir!"

"Hmm, honest. Line-up there and make ten rounds of the campus." I knew it.

No matter what I've said, this was inevitable. This was not the first time, I'll be doing the rounds. Happy birthday Miss Sara, you are going to have a perfect day!

I ran to the main road of the campus. There was one other guy too. I have seen him before but didn't know him.

"Overslept?" He whispered.

I had other reasons, boy. This oversleeping doesn't roam near it.

"Yeah! You?"

"Same!" We exchanged glances.

The whistle blew for us and we started our rounds. Everything was running into my mind like a treadmill, no stop! There was no fundamental thought, it's just that last night's incident was coming to me in pieces.

"You are Sara, right?" We were running the second round.

"Don't talk!"

"Why?"

"It will reduce my breath."

"Okay!" He stopped talking.

While doing the third round, there was no one on the ground. They probably left for the mountain and I was still running.

Around forty five minutes have passed and we completed our rounds. The trainer boy kept an eye on us. There was no chance we could slack off. After completing the rounds, I left myself on the ground. My bones were about to break.

"Gosh! I am tired." He was on the ground too.

I was taking shallow breaths.

"You are Sara, right?" He turned to me.

"Yes, why'd you ask?" I sat up.

"Um... remember you punched a boy in ninth class?"

"Yeah he was a senior, wait! You remember that?"

"Yes, he was my older brother."

Lighting struck straight over me, I froze for a moment. I slowly turned my head.

"... That was really not my fault, swear to God!"

"I know, he was teasing you."

"Ha! Thank goodness." I exhaled.

"What? You look... frustrated."

"Yea, I am getting birthday surprises one by one." I laughed a dramatic laugh.

Seriously! First, Siddharth being a secret thing and then that sleepiness which caused the late reporting time and now, the boy whom I punched once, his younger brother is sitting with me! What a great way to start your birthday!

"Is today your birthday?"

"Unfortunately, yes! How'd you know?" My eyes lowered my gaze in respect of participating in destiny's pranks.

"You just said that— and— happy birthday!"

"Same to you...um! Thank you." I held my head between my fingers.

He laughed. I looked at him. He does resemble a little to the guy whom I punched.

We talked about school and stuff and soon the squadrons came back, we stood up. The squadrons stood in formation. A whistle was blown for late comers to join the formation. We exchanged glances and went to our squadrons. He was from Shree's squadron. I stood in the line, beside Siddharth. My heart was throbbing as it would come out. I was screaming inside my head.

This guy, who is standing next to me, is not a normal guy. Last night he put me to sleep so I don't remember him and his secret but... damn this brain! I recovered every memory of last night. What if he finds out that I remember everything, will he cut a slit in my throat? My breaths were getting deeper.

Soon the dispersal whistle blew.

"Sara!" I heard him, he called me. God save me!

"Parul!" I ignored him and ran away.

He probably called me to confirm if everything was under his control or not.

"Sara!" This was Parul.

"Happy birthday future pilot!"

"Same to... um! Thanks." My brain was not working properly.

"Hey, Chemistry lover!" This one was Prashant. He hooked my neck.

"Late comer, happy birthday!"

"Happy birthday pilot Sara! How cool this sounds!" Shree came along with Nikhil.

"Happy birthday, Sara!" Nikhil patted my shoulder.

I felt like blurting out everything I saw last night but what if Siddharth finds out that my memory has returned then before becoming a pilot, I will be flying to heaven.

"Thank you everyone!" This was all I could say.

"So, what's today's plan?" Prashant was hanging on me.

"Nothing much, just a regular day. Trying not to get killed." I nervously laughed.

"Seriously?" Shree raised his eyebrows.

"Just a wish. Isn't it good to wish to not to die? "

"Of course it is." Parul flicked Shree's elbow.

"Well, see you at the school." We were in front of our buildings.

Parul hooked her arms into mine and dragged me inside the building. I turned my head behind before going inside. I saw him in a glance and he saw me too. He caught me looking at him. He was standing alone at some distance from the building. I hurriedly retraced my gaze and looked in front. God dammit! He got his eyes on me, he will definitely come to me and ask indirectly about the last night. There are only two ways, first ignore him and second, if talks, play dumb!

"Are you listening to me?" She was talking to me for the last minutes.

"No, I am not." I had to tackle the situation.

"Why?"

"Um... because I am thinking of something else."

"About what?"

"About... How is this day going to be?"

"Well, you should definitely think about it." She chuckled.

"Well, knock on my door when you get ready."

I nodded and opened my door. As I stepped inside, last night flashed in front of my eyes. I waved my hand vigorously to avoid thinking. My hands splashed the water on my face without any break! I am a mess! I exhaled against the mirror.

I slipped into the school uniform and knocked over Parul's door. She opened the door.

"Here!" She stretched her palms before me.

In her hands, there was a miniature toy of a girl with air-force uniform on it.

"Oh! It's so pretty." My mood was uplifted.

"I know you would like it."

"I do like it. Thank you so much." I was happy.

"Let's go!"

We walked to the school, in the middle, boys joined us too. While talking about random stuff we reached the school building but my mind was hovering over yesterday's incident. I went to my class. He was looking at me too.

I slowly shifted my gaze out of the window. He probably be looking at me every time now, one mistake and happy birth day will become happy funeral day!

"Sara! Happy birthday!" That was Aarya. She was jumping like a squirrel.

"Thanks, you remembered!"

"Yea... of course. Don't you remember mine?"

"Yes I do." Do I? My mind is totally busted because of that incident.

"Sara, is there something between you and Siddharth?"

"NO....no....why?" *Is it okay to panic?*

"Okay then but why is he looking here?"

"I don't know."

"Maybe..." Vijay sir came in.

She left my table and went to her seat. I looked at him, he was really staring at me. This guy! He will kill me with his eyes. The class settled.

"So students... yes Aarya!" Aarya had her hand raised. She stood up.

"It's Sara's birthday."

"Oh! Well, Sara, come forward!" I exhaled and walked forward.

Everyone started to sing the birthday song to me. A smile popped on my face, it felt nice.

"Thank you everyone!" I walked back to my seat.

"So, with the birthday wish, I am going to announce the monthly test dates!"

Nice gift, sir. Very pretty. My ears are feeling heaven after listening your words. I clapped invisibly.

"From the day after tomorrow, for consecutively five days, tests will be held till the lunch time and after that regular classes till the usual time. Chemistry's paper is on the fifth day."

I could not feel better, after listening this, I just wanna cry. It's first or last, doesn't make any difference. After studying chemistry, I just wanna cry! It's still a nonsense subject.

The class went on with its usual stuff and I tried to understand it. A bit went inside my mind because a lot of bit was trying to connect dots between what I saw and what Aarya told.

I kept looking at him in short intervals and our gaze collided almost every time. He was trying to kill me by his eyes, I am damn sure!

The lunch time came and so did the good time. Nikhil and Parul were outside for me while Shree and Prashant were downstairs. We ran downstairs to the outside garden. Dadi was there with some bags. A faint hope of seeing my parents lit my face but there were only dadi, Shree and Prashant, no sign of mumma or papa. I couldn't feel more broken. I was walking towards them with heavy steps.

"Boo!" A familiar voice.

Mumma, I turned and it was really her. Her embrace welcomed me. I forgot everything, every worry, every exhaustion, every fear, every agony and myself. It was long that I've seen her. My self was dissolving in her embrace, I was thirsty for this embrace. She hugged me tightly as I hugged her more.

"Mumma!" I was so happy.

"Sara!" She looked happy too.

My mother had short hair like me. She looked fabulous in the Navy uniform but she was wearing indigo coloured cotton shirt and white pants. Her watch was gleaming under the dim sunlight.

"It's been so long." I stood away but held her hands.

"I know."

"Dadi is also here. Who will come to her?" Dadi made a laughable taunt.

I hugged her too and touched her feet. She blessed me with nice words.

"Let's cut the cake!" Mumma opened the cake box.

It was a brown chocolate cake, partially covered in choco chips.

"Looks yummy!" Prashant could not control.

"It surely is." Parul had her eyes on the cake.

"Wait! Where is he, Nikhil?" Dadi asked Nikhil.

"He'll be here." Nikhil had his hands in the pocket.

"Who will be here?" I couldn't think of anyone.

"Siddharth. I thought, we all here then he should be here too. It's not good to invite him."

"Because it's awesome dadi! Let's not invite him."

"He is here." Shree hit me on the elbow.

He was coming here, he was approaching us. For the safety, I have my skills and this plastic knife which could cut this cake, would it? I don't know but I don't think he will do anything here as everyone is here. I don't have to worry and to assure him, just pretend! I nodded to myself.

"Namaste dadi!" He was being humane in front of everyone.

"Namaste! ...Look Archana, this is the boy I was talking about."

"Oh!" My mother's name was Archana.

"Namaste!"

"Don't do Namaste, give her salute. She is commander in navy." Shree was being friendly with him.

"It's okay, no need. So what you wanna become after your graduation?"

"Wing commander."

"Nice." Mother was praising him.

"Liar!" I knew his reality.

"What?" Dadi was near me, I guess she heard it.

"...Fire! I said fire...where are the candles?" *Narrow escape, phew!*

"Oh right!" Mother pulled out the candles and lit then.

I was looking at the knife and then at him. What on earth he is? All I know he was dressed like some Ninja but is he really a ninja? My brain was messed because of him. I wish I could kill him right now. I will happily take the blame as today is my birthday.

"Blow the candles and make a wish!"

I blew the candles and closed my eyes.

Please God! Give me strength to make a way through this mess, alive!

As I cut the cake, everyone sang happy birthday to me. I gave dadi a piece and then to mumma. After this, dadi cut a big piece of cake and gave it to Siddharth.

This guy had bewitched my dadi, completely.

Now the cake was among the five eating animals. In two minutes, the cake vanished from sight.

"The cake was really yummy." Prashant licked his fingers.

Dadi and Mumma were laughing. Dadi unpacked the food boxes which she brought as lunch. Different variety of food was there, it was going to be the best lunch ever. I went to mumma.

"Mumma, where is Papa?"

"Um... he didn't get a holiday."

"Hmm... it's okay." I have listened to this thing several times.

Sometimes I wonder if he is in some secret regiment.

I joined the scavengers for lunch. It was really nice. Aloo paratha, chole, besan chakki, poori, salad, naan and aloo pyaaz. It was just... heaven! We filled ourselves completely while Siddharth got his meal covered in this too. How could my sweet dadi leave that non-human high class bastard out?

After the meal, me and mumma talked about a lot of things. She told me about how things are going on the harbour. The lunch was going to end soon and with this thought, the bell rang. They only had time till lunch. She held my hands.

"I guess I have to leave."

"Mumma!" I wanted to tell her everything.

"What is it?"

My heart throbbed, *should I tell her?*

"Are you scared or tense about anything?" She read my face.

"Mumma... nothing." Heart was still throbbing. I forced a smile.

"Hmm... if you don't wanna tell me, I understand. You are a big girl now. Whenever you are scared of anything, ask yourself this, are you really scared of it? And then, act accordingly."

Her words got stuck in my mind.

She and dadi waved us goodbye, we had to rush back to the school. Everyone rushed back to the classes and parted ways. I was in the middle of the corridor with the words stuck in my mind which my mother said before.

"Sara!" I braked.

Heavy voice, Siddharth. Why the hell this time? Oh my god! He is calling me. What should I do? What should I do? Don't lose chill Sara or you will be a chilled corpse!

"Sara!" He stood in front of me.

"Yes!" I put a fake smile only.

"I wanted to..." He wants to ask about last night!

"Aarya! ...She is calling me. I have to go and if you are wishing me then thanks." I ran away and Aarya wasn't calling me. I just saw her at the door.

"What is it?" She was with her friends.

"Um... I wanted the book." Could've think of something else but...NO!

"What book?"

Even I don't know!

"Err... maths, right! I wanted your maths referential book for the test."

"Oh that. I submitted it to the library. You can re-issue it, I am done with it."

"Oh, okay then." I didn't know she had a referential maths text book.

The teacher entered and we settled down. Phew! I avoided him somehow. I looked at him, he seemed suspicious of me. Damn! All I need to do is to fight for myself but... am I really scared? Mumma's words were echoing in my head.

The class commenced and time passed. Till the end of the day, every teacher was giving the description of syllabus for exams. The next day was Sunday so we were a little at ease.

For the next six days, I didn't leave Parul's and Nikhil's side. I studied with them for the exams and after school in the library. In school, whenever I saw Siddharth, I just change my lane. In the class, whenever he called, I never listened. After the physical routines of morning and evening, he tried to talk to me but I always ran away on his second line with some excuse. In the worst case, I hid from him.

Everyone asked me why I did that then I gave them the lamest excuse ever.

'Mother told me to be nice so I am avoiding him. The less I see him, the less I meet and the less I have to be nice.' was my every time excuse.

I was ashamed of myself for giving this kind of excuse and everyone gave it a green signal as I was one of the freaky kind.

It's been six days of avoiding and hiding from him. Tomorrow is Sunday again which was decided for hiking.

Aarya and I were talking about things. She told me how the situation had gotten worse in the town and every time she is on that topic, it makes me remember about the night when I saw Siddharth in that Ninja dress.

During the evening routine, everyone was so excited for the hike. We played football this time. Our energy was totally drained out and I was bruised. After the routine, we were grouped again.

"Cadets! As you all know we are going to hike tomorrow. Report at six hundred hours. The squadron will be divided into ten teams and then teams will be further divided in three. This is not a fun hike, I want you to know that. You have to walk without trekking poles and with limited food and water. Bring your bags tomorrow. "

I did the maths in seconds. Right now in the squadron, there are twenty nine cadets. The place for cadet 25 is open. Ten teams means three members in a team and there will be one team which will have only two members.

"Further information will be given at the spot. Have tight sleep, now disperse! "

Parul was behind me.

"I hope I get on your squad."

"You never know babes! You can get on Siddharth's squad." I was totally joking.

"I wish so." Her face was lit.

I gave her a look. "She is gone case."

Prashant joined us too. "I wish Shefali was on our squadron."

Shefali was in the same squadron as Nikhil.

We all head back to our buildings while talking. Before dispersing, I saw Siddharth's face. He was somewhat frustrated and disturbed, maybe he was on the verge of losing patience. *Am I going to be a headline?*

It was six in the morning and we all were on the ground. I was wearing another set of track suits as the previous one in the laundry. String bag was hanging on everyone's shoulder. They were given to us for occasions like this.

Parul was behind and Siddharth was standing beside, probably boiling up from inside about which— I should give a damn!

"Cadets! We are going for a little jog. "

The jog started and after an hour we reached the famous hiking point in the city. We all were told to sit down for a while.

The trainer started to announce the squad member's name. As I calculated, there were three-man squads. Other squadrons were in different locations. The squads were announced.

"28, 29, 30" Parul was 29, she got her squad.

They had a logical arrangement but when my squad was announced, my life came out to be a joke and my own luck was laughing at me.

"26 and 27." I was the one with a two-man squad because 25 was vacant. Me and Siddharth!

I swallowed down my throat. This is the last day when I breathe. All this while I was hiding from this guy and this asshole trainer teamed me with him. God blast the trainer!

I slowly turned my head towards him. I could see only my death and nothing else. No emotion to be seen or sensed. It was very difficult to say that I could make it back alive. *God help me!*

A water bottle and two small packets of food were given to us and a first aid kit with one member. For emergencies or anything, a walkie talkie was handed in every squad.

"You have only this much to survive till evening. You have to collect the yellow flag from the top of the hill and come back to the foothill till evening. If you can make it earlier then it's good for you! "

He had the first aid kit, I didn't.

"Now three teams will proceed from the rear path, next three teams from the middle path and the next four will proceed from the front path. If it's an emergency, use walkie talkie to convey the message. We will surely receive the message and if someone plays a prank with this, then be ready with punishment! Any questions?"

"No sir!"

"Then proceed with your trainers!" There were three trainers to lead to the path of hiking.

We had to go from the front path where the sun will be on head in noon. We were all equipped and the squads started their journey.

After an hour, the sun was above and warm enough. The path was clear and intimidating enough to make us feel tired. Surprisingly, it was Sunday and a few other people were there.

Siddharth was walking before me. I didn't talk or look at him, we just walked. One hour passed, then second, then third. I was left with three fourth water, I was saving it for the evening. Another hour passed by just walking. It's been four hours and I haven't spoken a word, my stomach started to ache because I wasn't speaking. The silence was killing and there was no one around.

Other squads were behind as they halted for little rest but we were walking from the start without any break. The frustration was getting piled up.

"Hey you!" Frustration hit the level.

"If you wanna ask me about that night, ask me already! If you wanna kill me, kill me but— don't make me go crazy because of this stupid silence! It's been four hours and we are walking crazy. Give me a break from this tension and strain!" I nearly screamed my veins out.

He stopped with a jerk. He was four steps ahead of me, he turned and walked straight to me. He walked so straight that I took two steps back.

"Hmm... so you remember about that night. I wanted to ask but its okay, you told me by yourself." He turned and walked ahead.

What? What on earth just happened? He is not mad nor angry! How? I know his secret, I blurted it out so loudly without any second thought and he says, it's okay. Did he get fired from his job or something? All this while I was worrying about this particular moment and it turned out to be like this. This timid! I thought he would kill me because he had a different level of emotion that night— but he is all cool. Has something happened between the lines which I don't know? What is going on?

"Hey!" I ran and blocked his path.

"How can you be so cool about it knowing the fact that I know your secret? Aren't you gonna threaten me? "

"Nope!"

"Hein!" I dropped my jaw.

"Look! I am not a bad guy."

"So?"

"So... I won't kill you or threaten you. People in hidden villages know me, it won't matter if you know it too."

"What if I tell everyone that you are a ninja?"

"If you had to, you would have done it long ago... and I am not a ninja." He walked forward.

He is not a ninja! Then what was the deal with that kind of attire? And how is he confident that I won't tell anyone? My stomach has been struggling from last week to digest this information and he is dealing as if it is nothing!

"Hey! Stop..." *Why does he walk away every time?*

"You are not a ninja? Then what are you?"

"I don't think it's okay to tell a non-existent person!" I froze in anger. *What*? I gritted my teeth.

"You have no idea what this non-existent person can do!"

"Actually I do have it. A girl who doesn't think much before her actions, I can predict what she can do. Pointing flashlights on people without knowing is one of them." I stared at him.

"Why do you always have to boil my blood?"

"Um... I never do that."

"You know what... I am really gonna do it. As soon as we reach the school, I am going to tell everyone." I gave him attitude and this time, I walked away.

He held me by the back of the collar.

"If you do it, I will definitely kill you." His one eyebrow was raised.

"You said it before that it doesn't matter, now why this drama?" I threw his hand by my arm.

"I said its okay for you to know, no need to tell others!"

"Fine!" I shrugged and he walked away.

I ran and matched my pace with him. "If you are not ninja then what are you?"

"There is no need for you to know."

"I have a need to know. I want to confirm whether...
you are related to things or not."

"What things?"

"Some things." Mind roamed about the past accidents.

"How are the 'things' related to me?"

"It depends on your answer. Tell me!"

"You know what, yes you are right I am a ninja.
Happy!"

"No you are not a ninja, I know it."

He was dodging my questions. It was noon and the sun
was above our heads. The sun was bearable but it was still
exhausting. He kept walking away and I kept jumping
around him to get an answer from his mouth.

"Tell me, tell me, tell me..." I wasn't scared anymore!

Suddenly, his palm was against my lips with full force.
I held my breath and exhaled slowly. I slid his hand away.

"Please tell me!"

This time, he laughed. This was the first time I was
seeing him laughing like this. He looked pretty while
laughing. His eyes got closed and hair fell on his forehead.
My eyes didn't leave that view.

"What?"

"Nothing, just watching... Now tell me! "

"Huh! You are persistent air." He sighed.

My stomach growled. I haven't eaten anything since
morning. This guy was just about to say and this damn
stomach had to make noise. I held my stomach.

"Are you okay?"

"Yes, it's just hunger."

"I think we should stop for lunch."

Is this guy real? It's been four hours and we are
walking only, the rest of the teams have halted way before

and this guy didn't feel anything. He came into senses of stopping when my stomach growled. He is right, he is not a ninja. He is a high class bastard!

"Are you gonna come or not?" He screamed from a distance. He was sitting on a rock.

"Coming!" I ran towards him.

I sipped some water and then opened the given food packs and then, it took me away with betrayal. There were only sprouts. I kept staring at them, it felt like a dagger through my heart.

"Aren't you gonna eat it?"

"I was processing why they gave us only sprouts? They could have put something else!"

"Well you don't get much or nothing while on duty. Be thankful that they put at least these."

"Ha... I am very thankful that I can sell my kidney to them." I grabbed a mouthful.

He chuckled and ate his food pack too.

"Ya... you were going to tell me exactly who you are... so proceed."

"You are really determined to know!" I nodded.

"Fine... I guess telling you will be no harm but promise, you won't tell this to anyone."

"Pinkie promise."

"Okay... I am not a ninja, I am actually a hunter."

Chapter-6

"Hunter? ...Why that...ha! Aren't you... you are... you!"

"What?"

"Am I wrong or am I so right that I cannot believe?"

"About what?"

"Do you know?"

"If you tell me, I will." I took a long breath and held it.

"About the murder... which happened behind our building. A boy was found dead on the ground floor." I went too near him. His face screamed that he knows.

"You know!... And you know things which I have no idea about." I covered my mouth. "Oh my god! There are lots of things which I don't know, there is a whole another story going on backstage!"

"Your brain works fast on the things which don't concern you!"

"How does that not concern me? What if someday I become a dead body?"

"That won't happen as long as I am here." He got serious in his tone.

"Then— why did it happen to him?"

"Because— I was not there. If I ran faster, I would have saved him." He felt guilty. The guilt was all over his face. He walked away.

The air got strained. It was stupid of me to ask that question. It's my fault that I made him feel guilty and now I was feeling guilty. Only half part was left in the food pack. I closed it and ran to him. I was walking beside him.

"So... ah! Mr. Hunter, what do you hunt?" I had to light the mood up otherwise I would not be able to survive with that kind of air.

"It doesn't concern you so stop asking questions."

"Um... I had a question that totally concerns me. The night when you jumped... into my room, that morning I remember waking up in bed but don't remember going to bed— and I remember you putting a finger here and then nothing!" I put my finger between my eyebrows.

"Were you trying to make me forget that incident?"

"Actually— yes but it didn't work on you."

"Oh! ...but how do I remember that?"

"Strong mental power and will. Hypnotism doesn't work on those who have a strong will to not to surrender. For example, in your case, you didn't want to forget that piece of information, that's why you recalled it."

"Is there a probability that some things have happened to me and I was in much denial mode that when hypnotized, I was ready to forget and currently I don't remember any incident?"

"You never know!"

"That wasn't a straight answer."

"Because that wasn't a straight question. How could I possibly know if something has happened to you or not? I am not a magician!"

"*I am not a magician!*" I mimicked him. There was a pause. He glared at me.

"Look, we almost reached!" I stretched my finger to the top.

Perfect timing! I escaped from him and ran towards the top. As I climbed at the top, the view opened for me. Greenery and greenery, the other terrains were visible. It was felt as conquering the whole world. The air was nice and oxygen filling. I looked around, Siddharth came on the top too. There was a small table on the side, so I walked there. I found Vijay sir standing there.

"Oh Sara!" He saw me.

"Good noon sir!" On the table, yellow flags were kept.

"Oh Siddharth, you are here too!" He was his favourite kid.

"Here!" He gave me a yellow flag.

"You are second arrivals."

"Somebody before us arrived!" I was a bit shocked. It was tough terrain and we were walking empty stomachs. How could this be possible? I have a hunter in the team so we become exceptions, but who is trying to become exceptions?

"Yea, a few minutes ago. I guess, they didn't stop a bit."

"Surprising!" Siddharth was behind me.

"Sara! You know you should use this time as you are walking with Siddharth, gain some study tips from him for chemistry." This person will never leave me.

I inhaled a long breath to kill my distress. "Sure!"

I heard Siddharth's chuckling. If he was a normal person, I would have killed him. No doubt!

"Here!" Vijay sir handed us small packets.

"Nuts for the returning."

"Thank you sir." Siddharth took his packet.

We start to climb down.

"Well, we are on the topic so— I had a favour to ask."

"Ohho! Mr. Hunter is asking favour from a non-existent person. Speak up!"

"Ah! ...As you know my identity now so— can you take care of the school work like projects?"

"Projects? All by myself?" That was a pain in the ass.

"I mean— yea and I can help sometimes."

"No way! I cannot handle it and we got two projects in our hands right now and we will definitely get more. One more thing, I remember you saying that you don't believe in me handing the projects! What happened to that?"

He looked at me and blinked speedily.

"You speak very fast! And I know I said that but there is kind of an emergency on my side right now and I will offer my best help."

"Ha! Never, I won't do that rusting thing on my own." I walked away and chewed some nuts.

"Hey, wait!" I heard him behind me.

"Don't be stubborn and selfish! I am asking a favour." He grabbed my wrist and pulled me.

A jerk was felt through my body. The air rubbed itself against my skin and suddenly it became warm as I pressed my hand against his chest. My breath struggled. Everything got numb and a breath escaped from my lips. Our eyes met. The blood was rushing through my veins when I heard his heartbeat. My heart skipped a beat and I felt a garden growing inside me. I felt the heat on my face and then collected myself.

"Fine! I'll do it." I pulled myself out from his grip.

"Okay then, thanks!" He smiled at me.

This boy is such a bastard, high class bastard! I took my steps hurriedly and walked ahead of him.

After walking for few minutes, we found Parul and her squad. They were about to reach the hilltop.

"Parul!" I called for her.

"Sara!" She was out of her breath.

"Why so torn apart?" I held her.

"These boys... are... assholes. They made a run and I had to keep up... with them... so... "

"Ha... I understand!"

"Oh! Siddharth." She saw him. She stood straight.

"Hmm... Parul!" He was standing behind me with his hands in the pocket.

"Yes! ...Sara, water!" She was nearly begging for it.

I gave her the bottle and that bitch emptied it. I took the empty bottle in my hands and looked at it.

"Sorry... I was really thirsty." She patted my shoulder.

"Looks like that." I taunted her.

"You already been to the top?" She saw the yellow flag tucked on the bag.

"Yes..."

"Ya! Parul... we gotta go." Her squad boys called her.

"Gotta go!" She made a run towards them. I was still standing with that empty bottle in my hands.

"We gotta go too!" Siddharth called from behind. He was walking away.

I exhaled a long frustrated breath and went to him. After a few minutes, we ran into the other squads. They all were about to reach. The sun was above our heads.

"So Mr. Hunter... "

"It's Siddharth, stop calling me that."

"Nope!"

"High class bastard was better than the hunter!" I held my laughter but that was a very nice joke.

"So hunter, are you human?"

I kept pestering him with my questions. He clearly didn't answer any of my questions and kept saying 'No' or 'doesn't concern you' or 'no need to tell you'. I was a determined clingy type, still I concluded some of the answers.

He is eighteen years old and he is a human. He belongs to the villages hidden in the mountains of the south. He became a hunter when he was four, that's it.

Juggling my brain with him and poking him a lot, he didn't tell me what kind of hunter he is.

We reached the foothill an hour ago before the given time. I didn't have water as Parul soaked it all. I was thirsty, my babbling caused me this and my lips were dry. I wet them by rubbing my tongue over them but thirst was killing me. *When Prashant will reach, I will take water from him.*

We reported back and gave them the flag as proof. They took it and told us to sit down on the ground until the whole squadron came back. There were rocks lying on the side, so I went there and sat down.

"Here!" It was a water bottle.

I lift my head up. I didn't sense him coming behind me. He was offering me the water bottle. I looked at him and then at the bottle. I was damn thirsty.

"After chattering for so long, you might be thirsty."

I grabbed the bottle out of his hand and ignored what he said. After drinking the half bottle straight, I took a break. I inhaled a long breath.

"What did you say?" The voice was a bit distorted.

"Nothing! I concluded from your body language that you are thirsty."

"Can you guys do that?"

"Well yes, it's just about observations."

My eyebrow was raised and my lips were curled. He is a big fish. He has sharp senses, great observation skills, and excellent athlete skills. What kind of job have these requirements? Special and secret agents?

"What?" He brought me back to my senses.

"Nothing! Just thinking, with what kind of person I am sitting with?"

"Ah… nice one!" He chuckled.

"Hahaha!" I taunted.

Soon all the squads were back. I was about to give Parul a good beating because she emptied my bottle but she was all torn up and was looking pale so I spared her life. The sun was setting. A whistle blew and everyone stood in the formation. The roll call started. After the roll call, the squadron walked back to the school.

We reached the school and then dispersed.

"Man! Such a tiring day." Parul leaned on me.

"Parul! I am noticing, you are getting paler. Is your haemoglobin alright?" Shree was walking by her side.

I looked at her, Shree was actually right. He looks affectionately at Parul every day and notices this, her paleness!

"You should get your blood test done." I pushed her.

"That is not needed, I'll be alright."

We reached the building.

"See you at the dinner." Nikhil waved at us.

"I won't be eating tonight." Parul whispered to me.

"Why?" We climbed the stairs.

"I am not hungry."

"You... not hungry? I cannot believe it!"

"Really, I don't feel like eating...if I put anything in my mouth, it's definitely gonna come out. I am going inside!" She shut her door.

"Damn! She is really sick!" I went to my room.

I threw myself on the bed. Gosh! I discovered an absurd fact, he is a hunter.

What kind of hunter is he? And what is he doing here? Does he belong to some national secret service agent group and they call themselves hunters? What kind of urgency does he have? How will I do the chemistry project? Flow of the thoughts stopped.

When I said I'll do the projects, was it for both or only one? With this thought, other things came rushing in. The moment when we were close, too close. Huh! I collected myself and waved my palm in front of my face. What is happening to me? Hoo! Okay, in the end there is going to be a physics project. I should finish that and later I will clear out the situation with him.

I stood up in confidence but felt tired so I sat down again. He was again on my mind, what kind of thing he is? I thought I was afraid of him but really wasn't. I thought he would kill me the moment he came to know that I know but he was dead calm. He is the opposite and he is not as bad as I thought!

Soon the dinner time ticked and my stomach felt hungry. I went to Parul's door but didn't knock. I peeped through the keyhole. She was fast asleep on her bed so I didn't disturb her and went alone to the dining.

I filled my plate and sat on a random table. I thought I would be eating alone but Aarya came in time and joined me. She talked about certain things. There was a whirlpool forming in me as she brought up the mysterious events happening around. Soon the boys came in and sat around the table.

"Man! I am tired!" Prashant was still yawning.

"It was tiring!" Aarya added.

"I wonder! Parul didn't come to eat. Everyone is dead hungry and she skipped her meal?" Prashant was playing with his food.

"Is something going on with her?" Shree seems concerned.

"Why? Why'd you say?" Nikhil took a bite.

"I have been noticing her for the past few days."

"You notice her every day!" I took a bite.

"No, not like that. I felt that she is ill or something but she is regular at school. She looks paler than before as someone has sucked her blood out. Even that day, when I called her in the corridor, she just ran away and didn't look. Her behaviour seems weird sometimes."

That guy had a point. I have also noticed a glitch in her behaviour but I know how moody girls are so I ignored this thing. But as Shree is saying that weirdness seemed weird.

"Maybe she is missing her father. He never comes to meet her." Nikhil tapped fingers on the table.

"Yeah, you are right. I am just thinking too much."

"Let's eat." Nikhil acted as his big brother.

After the dinner everyone went to their rooms. No one had extra energy to go anywhere.

I went to take a check on Parul and peeped through the keyhole. She was still in her bed. She might be too exhausted. I came back to my room.

Next day, after getting ready for the morning routine, I knocked on Parul's room.

"Coming!" She was up.

She opened the door. She was all dressed up in a tracksuit and looked fine as before.

"You look okay now, what happened yesterday?"

"Nothing, just got a little fever because of exertion and lost appetite." She locked her door.

After the routine, we all went to school. Parul was fine so Shree was kind of relaxed. The routine has changed a bit and it's gotten rougher but it was okay.

As I reached the class, my eyes fell on him. He looked at me as he knew I was about to come. I smiled at him, don't know why, but I did. He smiled at me too.

"Sara! Come here." It was Aarya.

"What?"

"Don't question!" We ran downstairs.

"Shush!" We were near Vijay sir's cabin.

She peeped a bit and then patted me twice. I moved my head too and the view opened before my left eye. I could hear some things.

"We are sorry." It was Vijay sir.

"It is not your fault. The city is going through this, I don't know whom to blame?" I could see a lady crying.

At that moment, the first bell rang. We exchanged glances and ran upstairs. After stopping the sprint in the classroom, I took a breath.

"What was that?" I crashed on my seat.

"Remember the students who went missing a few days ago? That was the mother of one of them."

"She was crying. What does it mean?"

She came close to my ear. "Maybe one of them died!"

My eyes enlarged. "Th..." I didn't complete my word.

Meanwhile, Vijay sir came in. I tried to read his expression but he didn't show anything, it was all blank. I looked at Siddharth, he was also expressionless. I am guessing he heard us as he got so called sharp senses. Storm started in my stomach and so in my brain but I managed to keep my calm. The whole day went with my uneasiness. Nikhil asked me but I didn't say anything.

After school, I went to the physics workshop to make the physics project. With few items on table, I started my work on Newton's cradle. There were few other students in the group.

I put the base in front of me and fixed empty frames at the end against each other. I had five metallic balls and had to line them up with strings. I sewed the balls into the strings with my two hands.

Suddenly a third hand came and tied the knot while keeping the ball at its place. I looked up, it was Siddharth.

"You should've called me."

"It's okay I said that I'll do the projects."

"And I said that I'll help." I looked at him again. He sat opposite of me. I tucked the third string on the frame.

"I'll be leaving this town for four days." He leaned forward. My hands stopped working for a minute.

"Why are you telling me? Tell your friends, tell your girlfriend!"

"I felt I should tell you... and I don't have a girlfriend."

"Huh! ...What a waste! I thought you had one."

"Um... no! But I like someone." My body went numb for a second.

"Then go tell her!"

"I already did that."

"Hmm!" I don't know but I didn't like that.

He helped me tie the fourth ball. Our fingers brazed several times. Garden started to grow again inside of me at the first braze but he seemed unaffected. The wave of shiver was running through me but I didn't lose my calm. My face was burning.

"I wanted to ask this for a long time."

"What?" I was focused on the project.

"About the admission process. How do they assign sections and squadrons?"

"Ah... that! I also didn't get it for a long time. So what happens is that after all the paperwork, they arrange the squadron as per the scholar number but from the start, so many students left so now, they just fill the empty spot to balance. That is the squadron number. Sections are assigned as the alphabet you pick from the bowl." I always thought it was a weird concept. Our fingers brazed again.

"Why did you ask now?"

"Someone familiar is taking admission."

"Oh!" Another braze.

After the inside and outside struggle of a couple minutes more, the project was finally done.

"It's done." I sighed.

"I'll complete the chemistry thing after I get back."

"It's okay, I'll handle it." *Damn! I said yes for both the projects.*

I left the cradle on the table and went to the counter to register. As I turned, he was behind me with the cradle in his hands.

"Let's go!" He exited.

We both walked to my building in silence. I don't know why but there was this very weird awkwardness in the air. The news of death of a student was still in my head. The sun was above our heads. Two hours were left in the evening routine.

"Hand me that. I will keep it in my room." He gave me the cradle.

"Ah! I know you think that I am not capable of protecting people and the student who died yesterday was my fault." He did heard us in the class. "You don't know how complicated this all is. I wanted to save everyone but couldn't save him because I reached late as I was somewhere else, finding a way to end all this. Only if..." He spoke nonstop for the first time in his life.

"It's alright. I don't question your capabilities, you can't be blamed." I cut him in the middle.

"Only if I know this has happened, I could have done anything to save him." He was feeling all guilty.

"I don't know what you really are and what you hunt, but I can understand your place. I know it's not easy so—

don't drown yourself in guilt." I remember my parents' mission stories. He took a deep breath.

"Thank you for those words." I smiled.

"Then what will I get as a reward?"

"After coming back, I'll tell you what kind of hunter I am." He was at ease now.

"Really?" Old curiosity was on the surface.

"Promise." He gave me a warm smile.

"I cannot wait for you to come back. Okay then, I'll go make the file about the cradle."

"Alright."

I turned and walked straight to my building. I was feeling something different, it was new. Something which I never felt before!

Wait! What happened to me? This serious! I put the cradle on the ground and slapped both of my cheeks, hard. I don't look good when I am all understanding and serious, knuckle headedness suits me! Whoosh! I reached my room, swirling around with the cradle.

Gosh! He will be telling me his ultimate secret, I cannot wait to hear... but what about his other secret? Who is the girl he likes? Is she a junior? From another section? Hell with it... I don't care, but ....I seriously want to know.

During the evening routine, an unexpected thing happened. The spot which was vacant for a while, was not vacant this time. Cadet 25, was on the ground and she was damn gorgeous. Everyone's gaze was stuck on her. After the routine, we all gathered while going to the building.

"Did you see that girl?" Prashant was a bit excited.

"Yes." Parul was beside me.

"God! Her waist was so thin and features looked heavenly." I was zoned out. Shree hit the back of my head.

"Are you sure you like boys?"

"Ah! ...Yes I am and— she is totally a deserving candidate of my appreciation."

"I am having doubts on her!" Nikhil grinned.

"You like boys, right?" Prashant teased.

"You done?"

"Nope!" They all kept teasing me because of my detailed appreciation.

Suddenly, that girl jumped in front of us. We all froze for a moment and Prashant lost her chill. She gently stretched her hand towards me.

"Hi, I am Daksha. You are Sara, right?"

"You really know me or you are just good at guessing names?" I was surprised.

"Wow! Nice name." Prashant came in front.

We all turned our heads. He just lost his loyalty towards Shefali. We all had a disgusted look in our eyes.

"What? I still like Shefali."

"Really?" Shree hooked his hand on his neck.

"I hope we can get along." She was radiating.

"Umm...quick question, how'd you know my name?"

"Siddharth told me."

I remembered, Siddharth told that his acquaintance was getting admitted in the school. So it's her!

She left our side after the greeting. Our eyes were following where she was going and as a quite expected thing, she went to Siddharth. We were moving too but my eyes were kind of stuck at them.

At night, I couldn't sleep well. Thoughts were running wild and he was flashing in front of my eyes. She was so friendly with him. She was smiling and laughing with him and he was also talking intently to her. She even patted and caressed his falling hair in the dining room. Maybe she is the girl he likes. It was flashing in my mind by and by but somehow I managed to fall asleep with this much commotion in my head.

Next day in the morning, he was the first thought. I remembered, he was leaving the town for a while.

He left the town, I sighed. A sense of sadness crept over. When did he leave? This morning or middle of the night, I don't know!

In the class, when I reached, I looked for him. He really wasn't there but a surprise happened. Daksha was sitting on the table next to mine.

"Morning, Sara!" I remembered her sweet voice.

"Good morning! It looks like you are in my section."

"Yes, she is." Aarya jumped in front of me.

"I guess you already met." I went to my table. My eyes rolled over his table. Aarya nodded her head.

She kept talking about what they talked about but I had no interest. I wanted to know what kind of hunter he was so I was wishing that he could come soon. Vijay sir came and class commenced.

Next five days felt like a summer cloud. In this while, Daksha and I became good friends and I also completed the chemistry file. In this while, there were so many times when I thought of him. He just popped into my mind from nowhere. Daksha told me that he is a childhood friend to her. I wondered if she knew that he was a hunter but I didn't ask.

Another thing happened too. Parul's first love, Akshay called. That moron pretended to be his father. He wanted to talk to her but I cannot let that happen. Parul was too serious about him. She was heartbroken when Akshay just disappeared and dropped out of school. I cannot let that moron win against Shree. Shree is much better!

The school was regular and boring. Physical routines drain us every day and get us some new bruises.

On that evening, we all assembled for the evening routine and there I saw him. He was back, I felt relieved after seeing him fine. As our eyes met, he smiled at me and a smile too popped on my face. Suddenly, I saw Daksha jumping and hugging him. My smile dropped and I turned my head over. I guess its okay, if Nikhil was there, I would have jumped and hugged him.

The whistle blew and the routine started. After the routine, we were supposed to play football. Parul was on my team. We had the first set of matches and we won, no big deal. I fell a couple of times on the ground but that one blow which I took on my left shoulder was overwhelming. After the match, we were heading back.

"Umm... I am going to the infirmary. Something is wrong with my shoulder." I cut Prashant's joke in between.

"What's wrong?" Nikhil caressed my shoulder.

"It's straining. I think I'll get it checked."

"I'll come with you."

"It's okay. I'll go by myself, you look exhausted."

"I'll come, no deal!"

"It's okay, you go rest. I will catch up at dinner." I walked towards the infirmary, crossing the oak tree.

"Miss Nina!" I called for her.

"Oh Sara, come in. What happened?"

I went to the seat. "My shoulder is straining a little." I zipped open the tracksuit jacket.

"Let me check!"

She lifted my hand slightly. She moved a bit to and fro and checked it.

"It's just a normal strain. I am putting on the pain relieving spray and if it hurts later, come here once again." She sprayed it under my sleeve.

"What did you play today?"

"Football."

"Did you fall?"

"Yea... a couple of times."

"Oh... so that's why this happened." She taunted me like an elder sister.

I chuckled with squinted eyes. She asked me about the studies and we chatted a little and then stepped out of the infirmary after waving bye to her. I was near the tree.

"Found you!" Familiar heavy voice fell on my ears.

I turned my head. He was also wearing his tracksuit.

"You were looking for me?"

"Um... yes."

"Umm...I promised something to you but why are you here?" I remembered his promise. My eyes enlarged and turned myself towards him.

"Yes you promised that you'll tell me what kind of hunter you are. Now tell me, you have already heard this question a million times from me." He chuckled.

"But why are you here, alone?"

"My shoulder was straining so I got it checked. Now tell me, don't test my patience!"

"You ready to hear?"

"I am dead excited!"

"Well, as my word goes. I am...actually... umm... a demon hunter!"

Chapter-7

"Hahaha..." I laughed wildly.

"Enough with the jokes now tell me." Straight face settled in.

"You think I am joking?" He seemed to disapprove. I gaped at him.

"Are— you not?" My expressions changed too quickly.

I stared at him, nodded the head in a slight no. He also nodded his head in no. Atlantic glaciers took over me for a moment.

"You really are?" I just couldn't believe it.

I came onto his face, this all felt like out of the world. At that moment I was feeling happy, sad, scared and anxious at once. My organs welled up and my brain was sitting confused on the ground.

"Yes... I am. "

"Ha... .. ... " The biggest shocked reaction I ever gave.

"That means, wait... oh! That... it means... oh my god. Really? Oh, oh, oh, oh, oh, oh!"

"What? Are you alright or something happened? "

"Some things are making sense now but it's scary at the same time. That accident in my building... was... that a demon? "

"Um... yes."

"Do demons even exist?"

"I am a demon hunter so yes, they exist."

"Are you sure you are not kidding?"

"I am really not." He squinted his eyes.

Woah! I exhaled. My shoulders were relaxed down and my hands were touching straight to the ground.

"What?"

"You are so cool!" My thoughts reached the limit of appreciation.

"That's why you have skills like that! Your athletic skills are way too good for a normal student, I get it now." I was impressed. He grinned.

"Your reaction wasn't what I was expecting."

"What were you expecting?"

"I thought you'd be a little scared and in disbelief and maybe leave from here and hate me, but you called me cool, you really are weird." He scoffed.

"Let your thinking go to hell but you know what I was thinking? I thought that you are some secret agent and catch bad guys and your little group is called hunters."

He laughed after hearing this. He even stomped his foot on the ground to stop himself from laughing. I didn't crack such a funny joke but maybe from his perspective, it would be.

"I am no secret agent." His residual laughter distorted his sentence.

"Then what are you really?"

"Ah! Ok... I am from the Kayega clan which holds a respectable position in having bravest *Arks*. I am a white cornerstone."

"Hein! Dude, you just spoke an alien language. *Arks*? White cornerstone? Is this the reason your surname is Kayega? No doubt you belong to the mountains!" My brain just made porridge of its own as this guy's words were not from this world.

"Alright... I'll try to simplify it. See, demons are moon warriors so in order to face them we became sun warriors who use sun breathing techniques. Demons use moon breathing techniques and— the most skilled warriors are called white cornerstones or arks. The people who are demon hunters are categorized into four divisions. Yellow, red, crimson and white. These are colours of the sun and—don't make fun of my surname. They belong to the lost traditions." He looked at me.

I was looking at him, except for a few things. Nothing went inside my head. There was a big question mark on my face.

"What did you just say? Whatever you said was tougher than chemistry to understand!" I blinked speedily.

He sighed. "You really didn't get it much?"

"I mean... I got something but some things sounded too complicated!" I stood up.

"Okay then, I will... tell you the story of how it all started. Then you will probably get things." He stood up too.

"Why'd you do that?" I scoffed.

"I am taken aback about how much you are trying to make me understand things about your world. I mean...you can leave me with confusion and questions, why trouble yourself with the story? "

"My reasons." He simply smiled.

"I am kind of tired of listening to this line. *'I have my reasons'*, Nikhil keeps repeating this line and now you too!"

"Fine! ...I want you to know about this, that's why."

"And why?"

"That I'll tell you at the right time."

"Hmm... well, Daksha knows about whatever this white you are?"

"Well, the twist in the answer is that...Ah! She herself is an ark."

"What?" My jaw dropped down and touched the ground.

"What did you say?" I looked straight at him.

"Um... yea, she is. She belongs from the Saamik clan!" He took a step back.

"If you guys are this strong and everything, then why are you people here?"

"To match the pace with this world. We are not recognized by anyone so we cannot keep telling everyone who we are and to mix with the society, we do what normal people do."

"Then why are you here in this school?" My inner detective was on surface.

"Army schools are the best place for us to hide. Even by accident if we do something extraordinary, they ignore it by calling us a prodigy."

"Oh! ...Nice calculation." We started walking towards the building. The air was nice.

"So the story Mr. Hunter, tell me!"

"Oh yeah, right, the story umm...but don't interrupt me while I am telling you. If you have any query, save it for later. Okay?"

"Okayyy!" I skipped my steps.

"Well, it all started centuries ago. There was a wood merchant in the mountains of the south. He used to sell rare woods of the mountains. He had a little daughter, who was very dear to him. His wife died because of some incurable disease when her daughter was two. One day his daughter put her wish forward to see the ocean. The merchant couldn't deny her request and on the next day they went to see the ocean. They reached there in the evening so they had to stay for the night. They... "

"They stayed at the beach?"

"... I told you not to interrupt and they didn't stay on the beach, they lodged at an inn. In the morning, that girl went to the ocean before leaving. She saw a man in an unconscious state, she ran to her father and told her about that man. The merchant went to the shore and saw him. The man had some jewels on him and his robe seemed royal. He had a sword stuck on his waist which was tightly knotted. The merchant was a good hearted person so he brought that man home and got him treated. After the treatment, that man gained consciousness but things were different. That man spoke a different language. He washed off from other part of the land. He spoke different language. They both didn't understand each other but sensed each other what they were trying to say. The man was thanking the merchant. The merchant also understood that that man had nowhere to go so he arranged his stay in his house. After a few days, that man made a request to learn their language. He... "

"How did he ask him? He could not speak his language! "

"I was told that it was a struggle of an hour and— now save questions for later!" He sighed.

"That man started learning the language with dedication but there was one thing the wood merchant was curious about. Every night, that man goes somewhere with his sword without telling anyone and returns every morning. The merchant wanted to ask but waited for the right time. After some months, that man started speaking the language fluently. One day, the merchant invited the man over for tea. There, the merchant asked things about him. That man was an *ark* from a royal clan. His name was Ishmi Borko. He escaped into the ocean while fighting the *Purna* water demon. He was a demon hunter. He was the only sole survivor of the clan. What happened to his clan? It was never revealed. The ..."

"He was an *ark* just like you?"

"Yes, being an *ark* means mastering all the forms of breathing techniques."

"And you have mastered them?"

"Yes and I guess you won't stop cutting me in the middle!" He sighed. I put my finger on my lips.

"So... the merchant asked where he goes every night and then the he told him. He feels presence and smells the scent of demons so he goes every night to hunt them to protect the people of that village. It was his duty to protect humans. The merchant didn't believe him but didn't question him further neither stopped him. One day when a demon chased the merchant's daughter. Ishmi slashed the demon in front of him. He believed him and was very thankful. The merchant gave him a promise that till his predecessors live in this world, they all will serve Ishmi and his predecessors. After this incident, Ishmi established the foundation of demon hunters again in that village with original traditions. He found suitable men and trained them. He repeated what he witnessed from childhood. He gathered the information about the demons and did what he had to do to face them. The demons were divided into four levels. *Vardh, Ardh, Kub and Purna*. Then the demon hunters were categorized as yellow, red, crimson and white. As the name goes, so does strength. *Purnas* are the strongest demons and white are strongest hunters. White are also known as *Ark.* Demons use moon breathing techniques as they are moon warriors and hunters use sun breathing techniques as we are sun warriors." He took a breath.

"Later he got married to two ladies who accepted him. He had five children and later they were married too. All of his children were born with his fighting skills. They all became great warriors. The time passed and four other clans were established, Kayega, Saamik, Haara and Maisse. Borko is the root clan and others are branch clans. Daksha is from the Saamik clan. All these clans are known for having brave *arks* in the history. The merchant and his ancestors supported him and they support till the date... So did you get something or not? "

"Yes I did understand things but who was that merchant?"

"Have you heard of the famous JBB group?"

"Yes, that company is famous for its exclusive wooden furniture."

"An ancestor of founder of that company."

"Woah! That means you all are supported by that company?"

"Yes. Our expenses are paid by them."

"Cool! The current owner is dead rich."

"Yeah! I just got my monthly money."

"How much did you get?"

"Um! I should not tell you."

"Tell me! I'll tell you mine. I got a thousand rupees left with me."

"I got five."

"Awesome! Then you can give me treats sometimes, I won't say no. Thank you!" We were at the building.

"When did I?"

"You got enough money with you. You can at least treat me once in a while to keep your secret a secret."

"Fine!" He finally gave in.

"Cool!" I raised my hands in excitement.

The thought about my strain while hearing the story was forgotten but now I remember it again, with a red alarm of excruciating pain.

"Are you okay?"

"Yea, I will be." I bore through it.

We were in front of the building.

"I smell anger!" He said to himself.

"Saraaaaa!" I heard my name.

I turned my head and saw Parul running towards me. She pounced on me and we both fell onto the ground. She sat over my stomach and held me by the collar.

"You bitch! My father called me and you didn't tell me." She was gritting her teeth. She didn't look humane at that time.

"That was not your father!" I tried to calm her.

"Whoever it was, you should've told me. You know how much I was dying to talk to my father." She was so angry. I punched her face and I kept punching for a while. My shoulder strained and it was hurting more than before. Her face was bruised too.

"Why? Why? Why didn't you tell me?"

Suddenly Daksha came and pulled her from behind. She saved my life. Siddharth helped me to get up. A little crowd got assembled.

"Are you alright?" He had to bow a little because of his height.

"No! This time I am not." The shoulder was giving me a hard time.

Daksha was holding Parul in her hands and trying to calm her down. She calmed down and held her face. The punches were aching as an after effect.

"Daksha, to the infirmary!"

Daksha walked with Parul to the infirmary while Siddharth was walking beside me. She was a few steps ahead.

"What the hell has gotten into her?" I caressed my shoulder.

We all assembled at the infirmary in a few minutes. Nikhil, Shree and Prashant also came running there. Someone must've told them about our illogical fight.

"What happened?" Nikhil said as he stepped in.

"Ask her!" I taunted Parul.

She didn't look at me. The nurse was fomenting her with a warm cloth. Miss Nina took my hand and moved it a bit. It hurt like hell. I squinted my face with a great intensity that she sensed my pain.

"So now it's sprained severely." She sat beside me.

"You got your shoulder sprained, awesome!" Prashant made a lame joke.

I glared at him. "Ask about this to your classmate."

"Stop taunting me! You should've told me." Parul finally spoke.

"Give me a valid reason! Just because I didn't tell you, you'll kill me? And one more thing it was not your father.""

"Then who was it?"

"It was that Akshay's phone. He pretended..." *Shit!* Tongue controlling problem was about to create a mess. There was a pause.

Parul spoke. "I know that he left but I wanted to talk him and ask him something!"

"No you can't!" Unexpectedly, Shree spoke.

"Shree!" Nikhil tried to stop him.

"It's okay, if I won't speak today then maybe I never will— Parul, I liked you for so many years but you never noticed. I never spoke of this because I didn't want to jeopardize our friendship but today I say it, I like you!" A wave of silence spread in the room.

I looked at Parul and then at Shree. Things have taken an unexpected turn that I've never imagined. I always thought Shree will keep liking her until the time of graduation and Parul will eventually lose her feelings for Akshay but— the situation right now was much more suffocating than predicted.

Parul stood and walked out of the room without saying anything. Shree was still standing there. Nikhil reached his shoulder but he also left behind her. Everyone else stood there without taking a single breath and exchanged glances with each other.

"Ah! ...Well, that was... quite a show!" Miss Nina made a reckless statement.

We all looked at Miss Nina. She felt endangered by the collective gaze.

"I am just saying." She stepped back to the counter.

There was a room of awkwardness and weird silence. Siddharth and Daksha were standing in the corner. I looked at him, he saw me. He was not comfortable, I could say that just by looking at his eyes.

"Ah! Ah! ...my shoulder." I put on a fake show.

"Stop it already!" Prashant caught me.

"Okay!" I relaxed my shoulder.

"We should go." Prashant was at the door.

"Yes, we should go too." Daksha referred to herself and Siddharth.

"Take this." Miss Nina handed me the consent.

That consent was about giving me rest from the physical routines of evening and morning because of my shoulder sprain. I was out from the routines for next five days.

We all left the infirmary with my painkillers and consent and went in our directions.

"What should we do?" Prashant was concerned about them.

"Nikhil, I think you should go and talk to Shree and I will talk to Parul. Sara, you should go and rest. We'll meet at dinner."

They both left me with my pain. That sprain was killing me from inside. I changed my clothes after reaching the room. My stomach was empty so my feet took steps towards the dining hall.

The food was prepared and ready to serve. I was the first eater. I ate hurriedly and took the pills and went outside. The pain was getting more bearable, the pills were working.

After half an hour, Prashant appeared. He came running to me and sat on the bench.

"Why are you girls so complicated? She was sobbing! She is not going to accept him because she doesn't want to hurt him! What is this bullshit?"

"What happened?" Nikhil appeared from nowhere.

"Shree has entered in his all I-am-not-good-enough mode. He has stated all possible angels from where he cannot be good enough. I am so done with that boy!" Nikhil crashed on the bench.

"Listen to my case, yours was nothing! Parul knows that Akshay doesn't like her and she is okay with that but she is in guilt because Shree likes her but for some reason she cannot accept him! God save us from this mess!" They both were nearly screaming.

"And you guys left them alone?" They both took my support.

"Awesome!" I flicked both of them away.

"Well, I am going to try one more time." Nikhil straightened his back.

"Me too." Prashant stood up too. They again left me.

I walked here and there a little while rolling a stone by kicking.

"What are you doing?" It was him, Mr. Hunter.

"Nothing!"

"Worried about them?"

"A little." I sighed.

"Well you know...the story is still incomplete."

"You are still thinking about the story? Here the climax, plot twist, interval, everything happened at once."

"I guess this is not the right time."

"Yes darling! It's not." My tongue slipped again.

"Ah! ...Um... I mean, read the situation first." I was totally flushed.

"But... I have something very important to discuss."

"Whatever is it, come to me when we both are free."

"Okay but I won't wait for long." As he said this, he left. It felt like an ultimatum.

He is really a high class bastard hunter! After a few minutes, I saw Parul coming but she didn't stop and went directly upstairs. As she crossed past me without saying anything, it hurt me a little but I stayed quiet. She was surely in a bad mood!

"Did she go upstairs?" Prashant was behind.

"Yeah, she did. What happened?"

"Nothing. You should go! Parul is upstairs and Nikhil is with Shree, everything will be alright and your shoulder is also sprained. You go upstairs and handle her."

"Alright then, I'll meet you in the morning."

"Okay, sleep tight!"

I went inside and climbed the stairs. My mind was spinning because of all the things which happened today. Siddharth was back and he told that he is a demon hunter and Daksha is too. Parul came to know about Akshay's call. That asshole! I wonder from where she learnt about this?

A lot of mess has been made today, I yawned wildly. I was in front of my room but looked at Parul's door. I peeped through the keyhole, she was in her bed. It won't be good to talk to her right now so— went inside my room.

As I latched the door from inside, someone grabbed my mouth. I pushed the person into the wall, the grip loosened and I turned.

"Ssh! Ssh! It's me." It was Siddharth.

"What the hell are you doing here?" I threw away his hand.

"I told you I need to tell you something."

"Are you serious? You could have told me in school."

"I don't have much time to spare. You... you come here!" He held me by the shoulders and made me sit on the bed.

"How'd you come in?"

"The window was open." He drew the chair and sat beside me. I only latch my window up at night time, damn it!

"Um... this may sound weird but you remember the story I told you?"

"The demon-hunter-origin-history story?"

"Yes! That one. "

"Yes, what about it. You narrated me the story like three hours ago." *Three hours have already passed, shocking!*

"Yeah but I didn't tell you the whole story."

"And... you are here to complete it?" It was really weird.

"Um... yes! I need to complete the story. "

"Why? If you didn't do that you won't be able to breathe?"

"You can relate like that but I need to complete the story."

"Okay then, I am all ears." It seemed important to him. I crossed my legs on the bed.

"Ah... okay. Remember Ishmi— he was the grandson of one of the bravest cornerstone. He heard the stories of a demon to whom his grandfather fought. His grandfather told him that there was a remarkably powerful demon he had ever met. No other cornerstones met him much. The demon was expert in disguise as it used to hide itself in a medium. A medium is a person who is on the verge of dying and that person willingly gives their soul and body to the demon. As the last encounter with that demon was with Ishmi's grandfather, who died while fighting. It was believed that that demon is also dead but when Ishmi came here, he smelt that demon right away, how? We don't know. Ishmi ran several nights to find her and after a lot of effort, he finally found that demon."

"The demon is a woman?"

He nodded. "Yes."

"She has killed a lot of people and disguised in so many mediums that it was difficult to find her and soon— her trace of smell faded and was never found again. Demon hunters dispersed to different parts of the land in order to find her. It is believed that that demon appeared in the mountains, around two decades ago. It was the time when the present master's first wife gave birth to their first child. A widely known witch, Astra from Magazaan went to meet them. She read the prophecy of the demon hunter clans in front of mountain people as a gift. The prophecy showed her the future which she read loudly. The prophecy showed her that the third child from the second wife will be the reason for the death of the Selene warrior."

"Wait! Who is this Selene warrior now? And... witches? Master?" I was surprised that my mind was still working.

"Witches are real and Selene warrior is a demon. Her name is Kaumudi. Kaumudi is the most powerful demon in existence. Master is the person who have control over other clans and is head of all demon hunters. Ah! ...After that people of the mountains were happy and so was the master. After some time, the second wife was pregnant for the second time. It was night time when the second wife was in labour. The fate was twisted. The second wife gave birth to twins. The third child took birth but it was kept secret. When the night grew darker than black, the demons attacked all the households of masters with the intension to kill everyone so their existence is not harmed. Mass murder started and hunters fought with everything they had. Master fought too but the second wife was not in state of fighting. She knew why this happened so she asked favour from his brother to take the third child away from that place and nurture her."

"She was a she?" I expected it to be a boy.

"Yes, it was a girl. Her brother took that child away and went to an unknown place with his little brother. The clan was nearly destroyed but after the assassination of second wife and many other hunters, Kaumudi vanished in thin air and was never traced again."

"The second wife died? What about her baby?" My eyes popped out.

"Her brother felt that if the demons smelt the second wife's blood in her, then she would be in danger, so he left that girl in front of a house, but he always kept his eye on that girl. Before doing that, he shielded her with another scent so that her original scent won't come out, just for safety assurance. "

"And what about that Selene warrior?"

"Um... actually Kaumudi can only be defeated when Mandraak is there— Mandraak is a demon hunter snake. It is believed that only the third child can summon Mandraak after Ishmi."

"It is only believed... no one knows? Except her, no one is able to summon this snake?"

"No one else can, a lot of people tried but failed. That's why we have struggled so much to find that third child to teach her how to summon Mandraak."

"So where is that third child?"

"Right in front of me!"

Chapter-8

The words didn't process, instantly. *Whatt?*

A wave of shiver ran through me, the air got cold and I froze. Wild birds were chirping in the distance and everything felt like nothing at that moment.

"What?" I came back to senses.

"Yes... the third child is you, Sara! Your real father is the master, you belong to the clans of demon hunters. I had to tell you this, that's why I wanted to complete the story."

"What in the world this nonsense is? I am the daughter of an army man and a navy woman." I stood up with mixed emotions.

"No you are not, Sara! Fine, you don't believe me then ask dadi. She knows everything." His confidence was giving me chills.

"I don't believe this ...and...and... I don't want to ask anything from anyone. I am happy as I am right now. I don't want anyone to tell me what you just said. I don't wanna summon some snake or anything and I don't give a damn about that Kaumudi! Please..." He hit me on the neck. The more or less, I knew that sleep enveloped me.

The alarm rang at its usual time, slowly my eyes opened. I sat up, things rumbled in my mind. What happened last night? The chair was still near the bed. Siddharth flashed in front of my eyes and his words. I looked around, I was thirsty. I saw a piece of paper tucked under the water bottle.

I know that things are harsh but you need to think with a calm mind. It was my duty to tell you the truth and to protect you. Please don't hate me!

What a morning! Why on earth will I hate him when I already do that? Bastard! I laid back, my shoulder had noticeable hint of pain. My eyes travelled at the ceiling.

Am I really the master's daughter? Do I really belong to the world of demon hunters? Ha...! What the hell is happening? And... and the brother of the second wife? Who is this sneaky snake in this story? Ah! ....I need to sleep more, wait how did I fall asleep last night? I remember him hitting me on the neck. That bastard!

Things were running in my mind so I couldn't sleep. After some time, I tied my shoes and left for the school.

During the assembly, things were running wild in my mind. I was fighting for my own existence, whether I am a daughter of an army captain or the captain of demon hunters! Why is this even happening? Why did that bastard tell me that? I need an answer from dadi. Her saying is the only thing that matters!

After the assembly we all were back to our class.

"What are you thinking?" A soft touch on my shoulder.

It was Daksha. To be precise, Daksha Saamik. I didn't hear her coming to me. She didn't make any noise while walking. She was standing at my desk.

"Things, Miss Hunter!"

"Oh! So he told you. "

"Yea and with that he told me a lot of other things that I didn't want to hear!"

"It was not his mistake. He wanted to push this but we pressurized him. "

"Wait! We? How many of you are here?"

"Hmm, in this school, we are one hundred and six in total."

"Total?"

"Yea, you know the yellow, red, crimson and white."

"Oh yea! I remember that stuff."

"You love your dadi?"

"Yea, I do. She is the only person with whom I lived. My parents were always away. She is the person who wiped my tears and took care of me, and how can I not love her? "

"Master will be delighted to know how kind her daughter is." She smiled.

"Are you ready to accept your identity?"
"Tell me one thing! You guys are really not playing a prank on me because if you are doing this then it is way too serious!"

"We are not!"

Disappointment, disappointment everywhere!

"You heard about Mandraak?"

"Yea." Gladly, Aarya was out in the corridor as her red-house members called her.

"The Selene warrior, you know?" I nodded.

"Hm... he told me to tell you things...so this Selene warrior is very clever and is huge in size. Kaumudi rarely comes in her original form but when she does, it destroys a lot of things. She is so gigantic that we cannot imagine. I've read about it in chronicles. Mandraak is a demon hunter snake but he is not a normal snake or looks like one. Mandraak is as huge as Kaumudi and only the presence of Mandraak can assure that in the worst scenario, we still have a chance against her." I was listening keenly.

"Why anyone else is not able to call him? Why me?"
"Golden will."

"Golden will?" They keep using abnormal terms.

"The people who can summon Mandraak have a golden will. The will of sun. The will that resembles his.

Once the squinx ring senses the golden will, the Mandraak can be summoned on request."

"Squinx ring?" My expression was plastered.

"He really didn't tell you everything. This is the first time I am seeing him like this...huh...okay! Squinx ring is not a normal ring, it is the ring which senses the golden will. It is an ancestral ring which Ishmi had but— right now one knows where that ring is. The second wife's brother says he will find it."

"So in conclusion you people think that my will resembles to a snake? What if it all doesn't work out?" Siddharth stepped inside the class. I looked at him and then rolled my eyes away.

"According to the famous prophecy, you can— and if you can't— then we just have to keep trying and to find that person who can summon him."

"Is it tough?"

"Yes, but no! What matters is your will. "

"So how you..."

"Shush!" She cut me in the middle.

"What are you guys talking about?" Aarya was there.

"Nothing, just stuff!" I leaned back.

"Hmm... I met Parul on the way, is she sick?"

"Why'd you ask that?"

"She looked pale as someone sucked her blood away."

"It might be yesterday's effect!" I mumbled.

"Sara, why didn't you come to the ground this morning?"

"I got a sprain in my shoulder so Miss Nina gave me the consent."

"Oh, I thought you overslept again! ...Well Daksha, Nikhil asked me to tell you to meet him during lunch."

"Fine!" She turned to the blackboard.

Soon Vijay sir came in and class started. The day was just passing without stirring any interest because things were already stirred in my mind. At lunch, things were a little awkward. We were eating together but in silence! Nikhil was away with Daksha. I wonder why he called her!

Parul was not talking at all and Aarya was right, she looked pale and her eyes were swollen. She definitely didn't sleep properly last night.

While going back to the building. Parul made a brisk walk and went away first and Shree said sorry to us because of his confession. The group was kind of awkward. I could just say okay to him because— things were not okay with me.

The day went boring as Shree and Parul were sulking. Even at dinner, we ate silently! I was getting sucked by this whole situation. After the dinner we all went to our rooms without talking much but I didn't walk to my room, instead I went outside for fresh air.

The air was cool and nice. I sat on a bench and looked up at the sky. The sky was beautiful. The stars were twinkling in the clear sky. Things were flashing in mind.

"What are you doing here?" I heard Nikhil.

"What are you doing here?"

"Just for air." He was standing beside me.

"Me too!" He sat beside me on the bench.

"I miss the days when everything was fine." I sighed.

"It's been only twenty-four hours, sweetie!" He said it with a straight face.

I recalled, oh yeah! Things got puzzled from yesterday. Before that, I didn't know my real parents.

"Really! It feels like a decade." The air filled my lungs.

"How's your shoulder?"

"It's fine."

"It's been a while we haven't talked about things." Nikhil looked up to the sky.

"Yeah!... Do you believe in demons?" I wanted to talk.

"Yeah." His answer took me aback.

"This world is made by God. Wherever there is positive, there will be negative. Where there is good, there will be bad and where there are angels, there will be demons! "

"So you believe that angels and demons exist?"

"Yeah, I mean why not. If the world have this word in the dictionary, it means it existed sometime or maybe exists." Finally, a person was talking sense with me.

"Maybe you are right! ...Demons do exist." I sighed.

"Why? Why'd you ask that? "

"I read in library a little about Japanese folks. They got demons in history. "

"You still read those weird things!" He scoffed.

"You never know what kind of world awaits for you. You will never know about a person sitting beside ....or the boy who was your classmate... or was your past manipulated or not!" Nikhil laughed a little on this comment.

"Why are you talking like this?"

"I don't know!" He chuckled.

I was actually felt light after talking to him. The night had gotten dark and barely a student was outside. After talking a while, I left him and walked to my room and opened the door. As the door opened, I saw Siddharth on my window. *I think I should start latching the window during the day!*

"No! No! No! Not you again! I don't wanna hear anything else that could freak me out! You have already told me enough." I was totally frustrated by his sight.

"I can never get serious with you, can I?"

"Are you here to give me another heart attack?" He chuckled a bit.

"I am not here to give you any kind of attack. I am here to deliver a message."

"That would be a mind exploding message! Go ahead." Shallow breath escaped from my lips.

"Tomorrow, Master is coming to meet you!"

It took me a second to understand. Master! ...My real father is coming to meet me, tomorrow!

"Hein! ...What?"

"Ah! Yes...the master is coming to meet her daughter. He has waited desperately for this. For few years, he believed that you are dead too he knows everything now."

"It's that brother's will and— masters', not mine!" I was freaking out.

"I knew you would react like this. The whole thing is if you allow, only then he will meet. I am here to know your answer." I felt a jerk in my heart.

They are treating me like a princess but— I am scared. I have a father to whom I have treasured since my senses came and now I got another father who is desperately waiting to meet the daughter who left her side long ago. I am scared, how things will take turn from now on. What should I do? Should I meet him?

"What are you thinking?"

"I will meet him." Let's face this! *I don't know which father's courage is this!*

The decision was made. Things will turn fine, they will!

"Alright then, I let others know."

"But... I need to talk to dadi."

"Fine... I'll let you know in five minutes."

"Hm... wait! What?" I stood up but he disappeared.

I ran to the window and looked outside. I could see him running and jumping on the buildings. What the hell do they eat? And what he meant?

After few minutes, there was a knock on my door. I opened the door. Daksha was there.

"You ready to meet your dadi?" These were her words as I opened the door.

"What?"

"You said you need to talk to your dadi first, let's go!"

"Are we are going to sneak out? How?"

"That is our problem." She grabbed my hand and ran.

"The door!" It was flung open.

"Someone will lock it." She ran at great speed.

Honestly, I was no match to her. She had my right hand in her clutch. I was surprised, how fast she process things. She remembered about the sprain in my other shoulder.

There was no one outside, it was all dark. All the guards were out of sight. We ran to the main gate, there was a car parked in front.

"Get in!" Daksha went for the front seat beside the driver's.

I grabbed the handle and the door flung opened. The car was bit familiar but I ignored it. As I sat in, my eyes rolled to the driver. Siddharth was in the driver's seat.

"Let's go!" As Daksha said, Siddharth accelerated.

"You...you know how to drive? Or should I pray for myself?" My heartbeat elevated by the speed of the car. He was driving at great speed.

"Don't worry, he is a fine driver." Daksha seemed confident that it shook my confidence.

"Does he have his license?"

"Yes, he have the license and now relax!"

"Alright, if you say so." I said it but I was ready to jump out at any moment.

He was driving at such a speed that we reached in twenty minutes by clock. He clicked brakes in front of my house. Mahi's house was facing my back. I was preparing myself to talk to dadi.

"Everything will be fine!" Daksha took my hand.

I opened the gate and went to porch area and knocked the door. Shalu opened the door.

"Sara? ....Dadi! Sara is here." She shouted for dadi and her expression were she saw a ghost. Siddharth and Daksha were behind me.

Dadi appeared at the end of the ball.

"Sara! What happened? What are you doing here at this time? And Siddharth! ...Come inside *baccho!*"

We stepped in and sat on sofa. Dadi sat beside me.

"What happened Bittu? What are doing here? Has something happened?"

"Dadi..." I couldn't find courage to say anything.

"Bittu! Whatever is it, speak!"

"Dadi..." I took a long breath.

"Am I not your real granddaughter?" The words were out of my mouth.

"Who said—"

"You found in front of your gate and picked me up and took me inside?"

Dadi looked at Daksha.

"Who told you this?"

"Siddharth!" He was the one who told me.

Dadi shifted her gaze at him. He was trying to not to look at her. In actual, he couldn't look in her eyes.

"Do you both belong to those people?" Daksha and Siddharth nodded.

I looked at dadi, so she knew something as she said 'those people'. She looked at me, her eyes were about to be watery.

"Bittu! ...I knew this day will come and I have prepared myself way too before— uh— the things... what they told you is the truth. We did found you in front of our house— but you were the most beautiful thing which happened to me. "

"Don't explain. I promised myself that whatever you will say, I will believe it without any question."

"Bittu... "

"It's okay dadi." A storm was spinning in me.

She hugged me. I knew she was about to cry. She swallowed her tears.

"It's harder than I thought. Bittu, I know that we are not related by blood but you'll always be my granddaughter. You will always be my Bittu!" She was sniffling.

"Well now you know things then I should give you what belongs to you!" She got up and went to her room.

I was puzzled. What is it? Soon she emerged with a little wooden box in her hand.

"It's the squinx ring." I heard Daksha's surprise in words.

"Here! It's yours. This came with you and I was told to give you this at the right time and I guess, this is the right time." She put the box in my hand.

"Can I take it?" Siddharth stood up.

I looked at him but then gave him. He opened the box and his jaw dropped.

"It really is the squinx ring then why didn't I smell it before?"

"It would've been sealed." They both started talking in jargons.

"But I came here before. I would've sensed it."

"Because it was locked back then." Dadi said in between. "I was told to keep it locked."

"We should leave now! They won't be able to hold much." Siddharth said.

"And I will keep this until needed."

"Why? It's mine!"

"The ring gives off its presence as you are near it."

"Wait! Let her wear it once." Daksha took it from Siddharth.

She pulled the ring out of the box and put it in my hand. The ring was made of jade as far as I could guess. It was more like a miniature snake. It was spiralled into a ring. The ring was beautifully carved as a snake. I slid it into the index finger of my left hand. Suddenly, there was a shift in energy. Anyone would've felt it. What was that? What happened?

"The ring sensed the golden will." Siddharth had an expression of relief.

"Now, take it off. It got a strong scent, 'things' will sense it." He was referring to demons.

"We gotta leave now!" Daksha clicked the box shut.

I looked at dadi, she was looking at me. She did her best to hide her tears but failed. Her eyes could not lie much. I ran to her and hugged her tightly. I knew that she wanted it and so did I.

"Remember! This is your home, Bittu!"

"Always!" I faintly smiled before turning.

They were out in the car and were waiting for me. I bid farewell to dadi and assured her that even though I belong to their place but she will always be my dadi.

We were in the car again, I took a look at Mahi's house.

Siddharth was driving again at high speed but smooth. That boy had driving skills, I admit. Soon we were back to school. I could see some figures in the dark, standing around the school. They might be other demon hunters. I wonder what they had done!

"Sara! Run back to your room. I need to handle things." Daksha was in a hurry.

I nodded and then ran towards my room. They were talking about something before. They had to take care of the mess which was created because of me.

I reached my room. The door was locked. I clicked open the door but stood there. I peeped through the keyhole into Parul's room. She was fast asleep.

I went back to the room and laid on my bed. There was no sign of sleep in my eyes as the last two hours were poking my mind.

Next morning, in school, my brain and body were not working together. All I was thinking that what kind of meeting will it be with my real father?

At lunch, I wanted to tell everyone but we all sat together and ate in silence. I noticed Parul, she had grown paler. We talked about regular things but neither Shree nor Parul said a word.

In the last class, a peon came to our class.

"Ah! ...Sara, after the bell, go to the visiting room!"

That's it! The master, my real father is here! A quiver caught me. I poked Daksha.

"Please, tag along!"

She smiled a bit and then looked at the blackboard. The time was passing like crazy. The bell rang in a couple of minutes. The school schedule ended.

"Hey! Who came to meet you?" Aarya came near me.

"Maybe papa!" I didn't lie though.

"Oh! Say hello from my side. I need to go to library, catch up with you later." I nodded.

Daksha packed her bag too and held my shoulder.

"Siddharth is coming too!"

"Okay... I don't care!" I really didn't.

We hurriedly went downstairs by hiding and running. I didn't want to run into my friends that time. Surprisingly Nikhil went with Shree early and Prashant was with Parul. I saw them leaving the school. My palms covered the top of my head went to the visiting room.

I was standing in front of the visiting room. Beside me, Daksha and Siddharth were staring at me.

"You ready?" Siddharth looked at the door.

I took a long breath and rotated the doorknob. I saw a man wearing perfectly tailored pant suit and a lady, she was in simple floral sari. My gaze was fixed on that man.

He is my real father!

I started to feel cold, my body stopped responding. My brain was blank and my eyes weren't blinking. I forgot to breathe for a while. This is my biological father!

"Am I supposed to bow or shake hands?" I whispered into Daksha's ear and turned my head.

But... but Daksha's ear was not there. She had her head bowed down a bit. I looked at Siddharth, he was also in the same position. I stuttered in my mind, what am I supposed to do? So I looked straight. This was the first time I was embarrassed and feeling it.

"Heads up comrades!" The man spoke.

His voice was commanding and polite. Polite enough to pet a dove and commanding enough to kill a lion.

Daksha and Siddharth stood up. Daksha pushed me to the chair in front. I walked slowly and sat down. They both were standing behind as my bodyguard!

"Um... hello!" I finally spoke with no courage to speak.

"Your eyes are just like your mother."

"Ha! ...I don't know." I nervously laughed a little and made the trashiest statement ever.

Right now, I wish I was dead! That man laughed.

"I can understand your hesitation but as much I know about you, you are not like this!" He knows about me. God help me! Put some words in my mouth!

"I...I am... I am a bit nervous! "

"It's alright..." The man exhaled, he was probably disappointed to have a daughter like me.

"So... how's your school going?"

"Good! Just got my shoulder sprained." *Good*? *My foot*!

"What happened?" He leaned forward.

"I sprained it while playing football."

"Is it alright now?" He seemed worried but there were no expressions. I guess it is a demon hunter thing, Siddharth doesn't have it either.

"Children get hurt playing, it is a normal thing." Suddenly that lady with a melodious voice spoke.

"Here! I bought a cake for you, I am assuming that you like sweets. "

"Ha! ...Yeah, I do like them. Thank you!" I accepted the cake without any nervousness. *It was a cake!*

"Sara! They have told you so many things, right?" He was looking at me.

"Um... yes!" I cleared my throat.

"Hm! I know you will be worried and all disturbed after listening to those things but I am here to tell you that you do not have to burden yourself. Everything will be alright. We all will fight against them as we were doing till date. I just want you to be okay and I also know you might be shocked after hearing those things but I promise you, whether you could do it or not, you will always be my daughter!"

Silence fell in the room. He meant what he said! If there ever a statue should be made of 'man of the words', this man is the perfect example.

I could feel it!

I looked at him, he had a faint smile on his face.

"Thank you for the comfort but— I don't want to turn that prophecy into a lie. People might be looking at me with hope in their eyes. We will never know if we could make it until we don't try!" It came from deep within the heart. I didn't know where the deep of my heart is.

"You are really the pride of Borko. Thank you!" *Borko? Ah! The clan.*

A smile was on my face too. I don't why but it felt nice.

"I wish I could spend some more time with you."

"I am alright with that!" *My other parents do the same.*

"But I cannot, I need to meet some people!" He stood up and so did we.

We walked them to the car while that lady talked to me about random stuff. She was very careful about not bringing my other family. At the gate, black Mercedes was there, waiting for them. I didn't know that my real parents were rich.

"I hope we meet at a nice place!" His farewell style was different.

"Bye!" I was very careful to not to address him anything.

Soon, they sat inside and left. Daksha could not control her laughter. She burst out.

"What? Why are you laughing?"

"You should've seen yourself in the room. A brand new Sara was there, so polite and mannered! See, he is grinning too." Yes, he was.

"It's okay! Why stretch it? "

"Okay, I need to do something. You guys, go ahead." Daksha left us.

"Ah...Why are you like this...all crazy, wild and comedy-type?" We were walking back to the building with bags on our shoulders.

"It's defence mechanism! I can handle anything just by making jokes and doing something stupid. It comes from inside. Maybe I developed it from my childhood loneliness!"

"Ah! Hm...remember the time when you asked me that if you have ever faced a demon?"

I remembered it quickly. It was the time when we were talking about hypnotizing and erasing information.

"Yea, I do!"

"I guess, I should tell you then. Remember when you were at fun city and you couldn't recall what happened there and you said that you got memory gap?"

"Yess, I do!" There was a stretch in my words.

"Well, actually that day, you faced a demon. She made an illusion and you got trapped in it."

"Really! I don't remember that." My brows frowned.

"Because you don't want to. You were shivering with fear." He was walking with his hands in pockets.

"You were there?"

He bent forward a little to meet my eyes on my level.

"Let that be a mystery!" He had a grin on his face.

We were in the front of the building. I took a turn towards him.

"Though I don't remember it, still thank you for telling me and...did you really save me at that time?"

"Somebody did!"

"Then I'll assume that an angel did it!" I pouted and walked towards the building.

I could hear his slow laughter behind me. I saw him once laughing too loud, he did look pretty while laughing. He might be looking pretty now!

In the evening, I spent my time finding stuff about demons but found very little. I could still slack off for three more days from the routines. There were so many weird things written down in the book. Some says that demons are mythical and does not exist but some says that they exist and I am with the second crowd because I got demon hunter as my friend.

Next morning, while going to school, we all five were walking together. No one by mistake brought up the topic of those two. Normal stuff was our topic.

"Oh! Is everyone's project ready?" Prashant was walking backwards while facing us.

"Why'd you ask? Mine is not complete!" Nikhil rubbed his twitching eye.

"I heard from somewhere that the joint school event has been preponed."

"Really?" I stretched my neck.

"Yes, that's why I worked my ass off last night studying about medicines, just to impress Shefali! She is making her project on chemical compounds in medicines."

"You are one hardworking man!" I patted his shoulder.

"So are you with her?" Nikhil asked.

"Nope! I am looking for a chance to help her." He winked. Nikhil and I wooed while Shree and Parul laughed lightly. I pat his shoulder again.

He was overflowing with proud on his face.

Soon we reached the school and went to our classes. Daksha and Siddharth were already in their seats. Aarya came jumping to me.

"I found something!" Her eyes were shinning.

"What?" I walked to my seat.

"Look!" She had a paper cutting in her hands.

It was an article. I scanned through it and picked up the summary. It was about atmokinesis. I have already read about that.

"So what about it?"

"Isn't this amazing? Just think, power of changing the weather. It gives God complex!"

"So you want to be god?"

"No, I am just talking about its complex! It's cool. "

Vijay sir walked in and she went to her seat. At the end of the class, Vijay sir spoke.

"Dear students, there is an announcement. The joint event is preponed and it will be organized soon, so keep checking the notice board. So be prepared with your projects and only senior section will exhibit so, I am hoping best from my class"

Prashant was right, they are actually having the joint event early. His hard work of learning about the medicine won't go waste. I calculated. The files are done and physics project is done. Only chemistry experiment is left and he will do it. I looked at Siddharth. He was scribbling something on his notebook.

The second class commenced and day went with lots of laugh and fun. Everyone was dead excited about the joint event!

In the evening, I was again in library to read about demons. I still couldn't find something meaningful and relevant. I was so buried inside the pages that I didn't notice that it got dark.

"What are you looking for?" A low familiar voice came from my behind. It was Siddharth.

He came in front and took seat opposite to me at the table. He was in his tracksuit. All sweaty!

"Nothing much!" I didn't look up.

"You won't find anything in there. Whatever you want to know, you can ask me!" He leaned forward. I lifted my gaze up.

"I am looking about Mandraak."

"About him, you definitely won't find in it. It's been hundreds of decades, no one witnessed his presence."

"Then how can I summon him?" My eyes rolled.

"So basically, you are finding how to summon him, inside these pages?" He pointed at the book in front.

"Ah! Yea... kind of!" Did I do something wrong?

"You could've just asked me!"

"You could not summon him and I could ask you? What a joke?" I laughed at him.

"Then good luck with the treasure hunting!" He scoffed and stood up.

He got offended. My goodness! He never do this, then why is he throwing tantrums now? I guess I have to apologize for this so-not-offending joke and ask him how to summon Mandraak. He was about to cross the stack. I jumped from my seat and went behind him.

I reached the stack, surprisingly no one was in the sight. I am sure that I saw him taking a turn here but he was not there. Standing there confused and surprised there, trying to figure out where he went?

"Boo!" Soft whisper into my ear.

I jumped out of fear not knowing what happened. That unalarmed whisper knocked me over and I lost my balance. Suddenly felt a hard grip around my waist and another at my palm. I turned my head as my heartbeat danced as fast it could. It was Siddharth holding me in his arms. My body stiffened and I swallowed down my throat. He looked straight at me with his black eyes. His hair were on his forehead.

"I took my revenge!" He whispered again.

The sensation of him speaking made me shiver. His breath hit the crook of my neck and there I found myself feeling something!

He smiled mischievously. His whisper tingled and cause me shiver down my spine. He was near me, so close that I could hear his beating heart. His grip on my hand was getting strong and then I realized that I am still in his embrace. I jerked him off and pulled myself out from his arms. I knew I was flushed. My cheeks were burning.

"Fine! You win." I felt a little annoyed.

"Oh! This is the very first time when you admitted that you lost! ... How does it feel?" He made a little laugh.

"Are you going to tell me how to summon Mandraak or not?" We were talking in low voice.

"Yes but tell me first why didn't you ask me before?"

"It just didn't occur to me!" I scratched my forehead.

"Hmm... I accept that in your case..." I glared at him.

"... Ah! So— Mandraak can be summoned by mastering the seven emotions while opening the seven chakras."

I blinked. What he said? Mastering the emotions? Chakra? As far I knew, I was a student in army school not a monk! He read my face.

"Well, our body have seven chakras and seven emotions. You need to master every emotion while opening your chakra. As you master the emotion, the chakra is opened, allowing life energy to flow inside. "

"And how can I do it?" It all seemed complicated.

"By meditation. You have to concentrate on that particular emotion. As that emotion goes blank, the chakra will open and when it does, you'll know. "

"And you are sure I could do that?"

"Believe me, I will study chemistry in exchange. It seems too complicated!" I sat on the ground in distress.

"I have also done it. I'll help you." He crouched.

I looked at him. It was not difficult? Huh! Meditation? Me? We were poles apart! I sighed.

"I guess I have to do it!" I looked at him, he nodded.

"Tell me one thing!" Things clicked my mind.

"Who is the brother of my birth mother?"

"Ah! ..." He cleared his throat.

"I don't think I am allowed to tell you!"

"Tell me! It's an order from the master's daughter" I really don't know why I said that. He gave me a look.

"It's— Vijay sir."

Chapter- 9

My jaw dropped and my brain smashed itself on the skull. My eyes were about to pop because of what he said. Vijay sir is my uncle! I never thought of it but he was in this school from the time I got admitted here. My ears couldn't believe it.

"Are you sure, you are not mistaken?" I was hoping that things are not this complicated.

"I am not mistaken. He is your uncle, that's why he always keep checking on you."

"And still I am this terrible at chemistry!"

He burst into a mad laugh. Siddharth lost it. He laughed like crazy. I kept looking at him while realizing how much of a stupid statement I just made. After his couple of minutes of laughing, he controlled himself. He turned completely red because of laughter. He was looking pretty.

"You done?" I raised my eyebrows.

"How... how can you make such a statement after hearing that?" He was still laughing in between the sentences.

"I spoke what I had in my mind and yes, if I knew he was my uncle, I would've forced him to teach me more."

"You are unexpected, Miss Sara!" He walked slowly away.

"Wait!" I stood up and ran behind him. We walked to the building while showering him with several questions at once about the whole chakra thing.

"Look, I can help you but you gotta do it by yourself. Tomorrow is the last two days as the rest from the routine, after that you won't get much time so steal some time for meditation. Use tomorrow's routine time to get started on meditation."

"Um...Vijay sir or say my uncle had a little brother too, who is that person?"

"His name..." He bent to my height.

"I'll tell you later." He flicked my nose.

After saying this, he turned and went to his building and I was still standing there. I blinked speedily, what the hell! He said he will help me and walked away, what am I supposed to do? And why did he flick my nose? I scratched the back of my head while feeling a garden growing inside me. Books are the only thing that could help me.

I rarely saw Daksha from the last two days except in classes, she might be busy with her own stuff and I just wanted to avoid Siddharth because that guy's eyes and his face were causing tornadoes inside my stomach!

I spent my rest of the evening with heavy and lengthy books. It had everything I needed to know about meditation and chakra opening.

It starts from root chakra and ends on crown chakra. It needs a lot of concentration. To master the emotion, you need to focus on the root of that emotion and travel inside your conscious until that emotion becomes infinite at one point. At that point, all emotions dissolve into one another and become infinite. When that point comes, you'll eventually know that you have mastered the emotions while opening the chakras.

That was a heavy deal but I had to do it.

After dinner and chatting with everyone, I came back to my room. Things were getting fine and Parul and Shree started to mix with the group more but— for some reason Parul seemed weak. Prashant insisted her to go to infirmary so they both went to Miss Nina.

I jumped on my bed and folded my legs, resting one palm on the other and placing it in the mid of my torso. I closed my eyes and concentrated on my breathing.

I felt nothing, just heard the mosquito buzzing near my ear and crickets in the background. The food inside my stomach was not helping much and suddenly I felt the need to go to the bathroom.

After washing my hands, I came back to the room and took the position again.

Damn it was hard! In the book, it stated as it was rice plate eating but in reality, it was equal to walking in a dark room. I tried so many times to focus but there was nothing in the end.

"Do you really think you can do it like that?" The voice came from my window. I knew it was Siddharth. He was the only creepy-window person I had.

"Then how am I supposed to do... hunter?" I remembered his old name.

"Don't forget, you belong from that community too!" He jumped inside.

"The posture you made is not correct and plus the breathing pattern is not matching. Your hands are not supposed to be like this. Ultimately you have done everything wrong!"

I glared at him, high class bastard! No one told me how to do it and here I tried, and he is lecturing me!

"Listen..."

He suddenly held me by my shoulders. My body stiffened, he pulled my shoulder behind a little and grazed his index finger down my spine causing me chills in me. I could feel the warmth of his finger, penetrating through my t-shirt. He slowly pushed some blocks of spine inward, causing my back to straighten.

"Just like this."

I could sense him smiling at me but I was too flushed to meet his gaze.

"Here..."

He took my hands and put them on the knee of my folded legs.

"That's it. You are now in a perfect position. Now close your eyes and sync your breathing pattern with beats of your heart."

I closed my eyes but I was too much distracted as he was sitting near me. I couldn't focus.

"Alright! I got it now, I'll do it." I stood up.

"I am here to help."

"I don't need help. If I do, I'll ask you tomorrow!" I pushed him at the edge of the window sill.

"Fine! Fine! I am going." I could feel the heat on my cheeks.

"Wait! Are you blushing?" He pointed at my cheeks.

"It's... it's not blush, it's my anger. Now leave!" That high class bastard.

"Alright! Good night." Then he jumped from the window.

As he went away, I shut my window down and latched it. A long and relaxed breath escaped from my lips. I touched my cheeks, they were burning. Why on earth? Why? Why am I feeling this? I slapped myself. I have to concentrate, I'll do it!

The school was getting prepared for the upcoming joint event. Students were crazy excited about this. Evening routine time was turned to March past practice time.

With this, I kept up with the meditation thing. After spending a lot of time with closed eyes and after seven days of hardship, I was able to open my root chakra while mastering the emotion, fear.

It felt some holy experiment but I did it in my own way. My root chakra has opened now!

In these seven days, Siddharth pestered me a lot. I don't know why but whenever he was near, my heart beats went crazy and cheeks turn red. Butterflies flutter their wings inside my stomach and I really feel annoyed because of this feeling. I somewhat liked it but hated it too. I am supposed to hate this guy but I sometimes laughed at his lame jokes.

Slowly and gradually, I opened sacral, naval, heart, throat, third eye and crown chakra while mastering sadness, anger, disgust, contempt, surprise and happiness. All these emotions just came to me after opening the root chakra. Crown chakra somewhat took time but in the end, I had it too. Daksha and Siddharth were a big help through this but my heart acted crazier around Siddharth, from the last five days.

It happened when I was trying to open my crown chakra. He was sitting beside, helping me to sync my breathing pattern but then an ant bit me in the toe. I got surprised by this sudden attack and cried in pain. I didn't realize how close he was sitting and my little stumbling caused him disbalance and we kind of fell on the floor. He was over me while my hand was hooked onto his shoulders. It was all very awkward and blood rushing. I could hear his beating heart inside his chest, wanting to jump out and beat. That was the first time my heart fluttered so fast that I could die because of that. My skin was burning and cheeks became red.

His black eyes had tornadoes inside while mine was seeking a place to settle!

Even today when Vijay sir took our names together, my heart went wild again. The only thing I knew was that my heart is never going to be the same again as before. Maybe I have fallen for him, a little!

"Sara!" Aarya broke my streak of thoughts.

"Yes baby!"

"Did you read today's newspaper?" She came to my seat.

"No! Why? Did you become Miss Universe? "

"No, stupid! ...I read that last night, a house in tenth sector with family of seven people were found dead. They were killed and only partial bodies were recovered, not the full body!"

"Oh god! Seriously!" I had disgust and anger at peaks.

"Yea! People say that it's an animal doing but some say that the killer did it. Ah! ....I don't know what has happened to this world? It leaves me disgusted from head to toe!"

"This is the first case of this month I am listening to!"

"Duuddee! You really live in your own world. Lot of people and animals were missing and killed. Generally young boys and girls were killed but the good thing is that a lot of them were saved too! It all happens at the town. We should be lucky that we live on the outskirts!"

The English teacher stepped in. She quietly went to her seat. We exchanged glances and then looked straight at the blackboard.

The joint event was after two days so after today, the school will remain closed. Two days are needed for other preparation and arrangements. Around hundred students were coming from the sister school. There are going to be various events like singing, dancing, drama, sports matches, exhibitions and many things. The joint event lasted for five days. These days are the best five days of the whole year.

As the school bell rang for dismissal, everyone cheered loudly in excitement. For the next week, there is no physical routine or classes, what could a student ask for more?

After the dismissal of school, I went to Siddharth to ask about the chemistry experiment.

"You don't worry about that, your uncle is on our side!" He winked playfully.

"He is my uncle not yours!"

"But I am yours!"

"What?" I could instantly feel the heat on my cheeks.

"I mean, I am on your team. I am your team." I could figure out a hidden smile on his face!

He was definitely teasing me as he saw how flushed I was. I gave him a look and turned on my heels. I picked my bag and went outside of the class where Nikhil was waiting for me.

"What makes you look this annoyed?" Nikhil asked while walking.

"There are some people who do this to me!"

"Did you fight with Siddharth again?"

"No... not really. I mean he mistakenly said something which was awkward and later he teased me about it." I clearly hid my side of the story.

"And what did he say?" Nikhil was getting on my nerves.

"Leave it... I don't wanna spoil my mood."

"Hmm yes... did you know Siddharth is kind of famous in the ninth class of junior section?"

"Why? What did he do?" He was already much famous among girls.

"Yesterday, in school, a girl from that class fell from the stairs and twisted her ankle badly. Luckily we both were discussing something with Vijay sir and saw it. She was badly hurt so Siddharth picked her in his arms and took her to the infirmary. After this, all the girls kind of circled him and talked about so many things and thanked him like a million times."

My blood boiled under my veins. This time I was angry, so angry that I could twist the other ankle of that girl and punch teeth out of all those girls who tried to hit on him. I could feel the disbalance of my emotions and my chakras. I clenched my fingers in fist.

"Sara! Do you know that that girl was kinda cute, even Prashant admitted. I guess if she tries and Siddharth agrees, they can be a pretty good couple!"

"Stop! Stop there right now!" I nearly screamed at him. I took a long breath.

"Don't talk about it anymore! Okay?" Anger was dripping from my words.

"Alright!" He casually said that. We were about to reach the building.

After a pause, Nikhil opened his mouth again.

"You like Siddharth, don't you?" I froze on his words.

"N... no! I was... I was pissed at him and didn't want to hear his name."

"Oh... liar! I knew it, you stuttered. You like him and that's why you clenched your fingers when I told you about it."

"I did not!" I shouted at him and ran to my building.

I ran and stopped directly at my room. Parul was not there as she was busy in preparations and so were Prashant and Shree. Luckily, these three were not with us! If they were, I would've blurted out the fact.

I pressed my chest against the heart, it was beating too fast. I've started to feel too much!

A knock on my door. It was Parul. She was back from school.

From the last few days, everything was getting normal. We all were getting to what we were at the start. Prashant was still chasing Shefali and Shree and Parul started to talk again for the sake of old good times but Parul got changed. She spoke less but one thing stayed same, bickering with Prashant.

She settled in my room while doing some paperwork for the arrangement. I was laying in my bed reading comics.

In the evening, I was summoned along some other students to the ground to make boundaries of the ground by *choona*.

After the hard work of hours, the ground was done. Hunger kicked in and I ran to the dinner hall. Everyone already ate so I ate with the students who were with me at the ground. Soon dinner was finished too and I was back in the room to relax.

I kicked my shoes out and folded my legs on the floor and started to concentrate on my breathing pattern. I had to strengthen the structure of opened chakras with balanced emotions inside me. In the next five minutes, all the chakras were opened. I could feel the flow of energy inside me. It was just like a perfect sunny day of autumn.

"You have done a very good job!"

Siddharth was again at my window. I slowly opened my eyes without disturbing the flow of energy. I rolled my eyes at him.

"I know!"

"Hmm... you seem confident in yourself. Let's test it!" He jumped inside my room.

"What do you mean by that?" I frowned.

"Let's try summoning Mandraak!"

"What?" My jaw dropped.

"Yes! I mean, you did all this to summon him. Let's try then and your chakras are opened too with mastered emotions. You can almost maintain balance between everything so..."

It wasn't a bad idea. After all, I did this to summon Mandraak. Should I give it a try? What worse could happen? He won't be summoned, that's it!

"Okay but where?" I was dead ready for this.

"Little bit far from here but first wear this..." He took out something from his pocket.

It was that same wooden box which had the squinx ring inside. I opened it, the ring was illuminating as always. I wore it on my index finger.

"Let's go!" He grabbed my wrist and ran out of my room.

"The care-taker is still on the gate, did you handle her?" I remembered while rushing down the stairs.

"No not really! This time, I have no plans. "

"What?" I braked my feet.

"I have a way." He said in an assuring way.

We were on the first floor where he took the turn to the end of the corridor. It was dead silent. I ran on my toes to him.

"Why did you turn here?" He shushed me.

I gave him a look. If he was not the guy I liked, I would have chopped his head right now!

He went at the end. There was a big window for ventilation in the corridor. He slightly opened it and pushed the grill up.

"Are we gonna jump from there?" My eyes were wide open.

"Well I am gonna— and you are going to climb on me." He winked. I could see that much from the corridor's light.

I raised my brow and gave him 'are you serious?' look but he was serious. He bent his knees a little while facing me backwards. Gosh! This is going to be awkward for me. I could already feel the rushing blood in my veins. I hopped on his back. Man! I could have died because of that throbbing. I was not suffocated but still could not breathe. His hands lightly grazed against my skin and tucked themselves under my knees. I was going crazy and then he whispered to me.

"Hold on tight!"

His low voice showered chills down my spine as he whispered. Hair on my skin was fighting to stand upright. I was into my thoughts and didn't notice when he jumped and before I could realize, my jaw crashed into his shoulder. I groaned in pain.

"Is your shoulder made of rock?" I rubbed my jaw.

"Couldn't you stiff yourself?"

"You could have alarmed before jumping!"

"Couldn't you see the stance when I was about to jump? You study in army school not in drama school!"

"Fine! I didn't see but you could have said it to me once!"

"Sara! I did say." I could sense him smiling.

"What?" I was still annoyed because of the pain and then remembered then he told me to hold tight. I realized mistake on my part.

"...Now hold on tight because I am going to run."

"Fi..." I couldn't completely say fine.

He was fast. His speed was nothing like a human. The air was ripping my skin. I heard him mumbling.

"Intense breathing... "

I don't know what the hell he meant but with that speed, I was surely be thrown on the ground. He shifted his whole weight on his fore body. He was too fast.

My eyes were struggling to open themselves against that much force of air. After struggling for a minute or two, he stopped. My whole body was shaking. Ants were crawling under my skin.

"Are you alright?" He surely saw my condition.

"No... I am not! Do you have boosters in your feet? Who the hell run so fast? My face would have been torn by the pressure of the air!" I was scolding with my residual energy.

He took a long breath but he wasn't exhausted much. That was great surprise!

"You could have buried your face into my back."

"I didn't get time to collect myself." I was on the ground.

I looked around. It wasn't a familiar place. There was nothing to be seen for kilometres. It was a massive ground.

"What place is this?"

"This... this is barren ground, outside the city."

My eyes widened. Outside the city! He came out of the city in a minute! We were at the outskirts a minute ago.

"Did... did you... really?" My words were stuck down my throat.

"Yeah, I... came out the whole town."

"In few minutes?" My eyes were about to pop out.

"Our bodies are habitual of running at this speed. With right breathing pattern, anyone can do this. "

"Whatever!" Huh! He was showing off.

Suddenly I felt a sting in finger. Blood was oozing out of my finger and the ring was covered in blood.

"How did...?"

"Don't worry! The squinx ring has sensed the golden will. It made a connection to Mandraak with your blood. It's a sign that you have opened chakras."

"So from now on, every time when I'll wear this, the ring will do the bloodbath?"

"Yes!" He chuckled.

"Huh, the blood is dripping out of my hands. I don't like this, I have this intense urge to wipe it out. "

"Ah! Now go and sit in the middle of the ground. Balance your emotions with chakras and make a polite request to Mandraak to appear. "

"Request?"

"Yea... on request, 'Lord Mandraak' will appear. While requesting to him that it's you."

"Lord?"

"Yeah, he is a lord."

"What am I supposed to request?"
"Just say that you want Lord Mandraak to appear."

"That's it!" I didn't know that the request would be this informal.

"Yes! Now go." He pushed me to middle of the ground.

I walked down to some distance and sat down. I made the stance of meditation and balanced my emotions with opened chakras and made a so-called polite request.

I, Sara, requests Lord Mandraak to appear!

I exhaled and opened my eyes slowly. There was nothing in front. I shouted at Siddharth.

"See, I was not sure and you forced me... "

Suddenly I felt a loud and pressurizing hiss all over me. The wave of air was strong, strong enough to knock me over. Chills ran through my whole body. I gathered my guts and turned my head.

As I turned, chills intensified. I was looking directly into his eyes.

Mandraak was in front of me. He was massive, so massive that I was not to capture him fully in my eyes. His aura was ominous than a dragon. No wonder he was needed to kill Kaumudi. His golden eyes were bigger than my whole body. The barren land was right amount of space needed him to settle. He was above my head. His black snake skin seem harder than iron. I was feeling so much emotions at one time because I was at the point where all emotion became one.

"So this is Lord Mandraak!" Siddharth was in total awe.

I stretched my hand and placed it between his eyes. He was calm. I could feel it.

"You have surpassed every demon hunter in our history." Siddharth came towards me. He himself was looking at him in awe. "You have befriended him."

"Greetings to Lord Mandraak." He bowed to him.

Mandraak lifted his head straight to the sky. He looked like a skyscraper. He was wavering in his coil and I was awe.

"...Prophecy seems to be true." Siddharth put his hand on my shoulder.

"I did it! I did it! Siddharth, I did it! I summoned Mandraak!" I was jumping happily. I grabbed him by the shoulder and shook him. I was repeating it like parrot.

"Look at him, he is so enormous." I was still looking at Mandraak with an ocean of amazement in my eyes.

Mandraak slowly got down, coiled us inside his tail and put his head near us on the ground.

"What does it mean?" I didn't get his this position.

"A gesture of friendship, he is comfortable around you!" He shrugged his shoulders.

A smile popped on my face. Was I capable of something like this? I didn't know that!

"Well, you need you need to send him back and I am happy that you are this much happy!" He freed himself from my clutch.

"How am I supposed to do that?" My brows frowned.

"You have to request politely to depart for home."

"Hm... I'll try."

I took my position again and closed my eyes.

I, Sara, requests Lord Mandraak to depart for his home.

My eyes opened and then suddenly I felt buckets of water over me.

Completely soaked into water.

I looked up, Mandraak was not there anymore and the whole ground was soaked. I heard Siddharth's laughing from behind. I looked at him, his clothes were dry.

"Whenever Mandraak disappears, he goes with traces of water bubbles behind him. He lives in the ocean— and it looks like one of the trace fell on you."

"It is a good thing, I mean I was able to summon Mandraak. Not like you, who couldn't even do this."

"That is because you are that person of prophecy, if you weren't, even you couldn't have done that!"

"Excuses and excuses, it needs determination and you lack it." I flipped my hair to get some water out.

Suddenly he grabbed my wrist and pulled me. I turned to him. Some water was on his face. My giggle escaped. He took a long breath.

"Sara...isn't the moon lovely?"

He said it in low and calm voice. His eyes gleamed under the moon. The air around us enveloped itself into something deep and warm. I could hear his heartbeat elevating as he said it. My heart was going crazy too as I was close to him. Everything around me faded into nothing as I all could look was his eyes. His eyes were ethereal. Those pitch black eyes had so much in it. A sigh escaped from my lips in admiration.

"Yes!"

I didn't know why he said that but the moon looked really lovely. He chuckled and moved some strands of hair away from my face. He tucked them behind my ear and let my wrist go. My cheeks were on fire. I didn't understand what happened but played along and pulled myself back.

"We should head back."

I hopped on his back and in next few minutes, I was again at my room. He ran a bit slow this time.

Next day the preparations were on its peak. The whole school was decorated by paintings, origami, and curtains. We practiced marching and other activities. Arrangements for stay were made. The ground was cleaned again and participants for different activities finalized their performance. Projects for the exhibition were gathered and the food arrangements were organized for the coming students. The whole day went into arrangements and I kept running from here and there. I didn't had a second to think about last night.

At the end of the day, I just wanted to lay down on my bed and sleep. Vijay sir gave me the task to paste the code numbers on the desk where projects will be displayed. I took the list from his hands. He was about to leave.

"Sir!" I wanted to tell him.

"Yes Sara!"

"Sir... I wanted to say something!"

"Yes!" I became silent for a minute then took a long breath.

"Sir... I ....I know that you are my uncle, brother of my birth mother." I said it in one go. He turned to me.

"I know!" He smiled warmly.

"I want to thank you for saving my life at that time." I was nervously making circles on the table.

"I had to, you are my only niece." He patted my head.

"You are the child from the prophecy, I guess you know your responsibility?"

"Yes... uncle!" I smiled childishly. He smiled too.

"Uncle... who is your little brother?" Siddharth didn't tell me at that time.

"You don't know? I thought you knew!"

"No tells me anything completely... they just leave things in suspense!" I pouted. Vijay sir laughed.

"Well... Nikhil is my little brother."

Chapter-10

"What?" My shocked face was like a confused lamb.

"Yes! Nikhil is my brother and in fact he is your uncle too. He is also an *ark*."

Breaking news for me, *my best friend became my uncle!* My brain couldn't process it.

He was laughing at my reaction.

"It's alright! Give time to sync that and paste all the codes on the table at the earliest." Then he left for some other work.

I was still standing there, dazed! All this time I was being crazy and wild with my uncle! He was a bit older than me and whenever I asked him why he is studying behind his age group then he always said that his admission was late, oh my god! All those crappy excuses are making sense now. Whenever he got bruised badly, he always said that he had his reasons! My hands rested on my head as everything made sense!

"Sara!" A heavy whisper.

I was startled and completely lost my balance. I stumbled and my heels got spun and I was about to fall down. My hands were searching to grab something. Suddenly I felt a grip on my wrist. Fingers so soft yet dominating, a touch so rough but still polite. My body stiffened as I grabbed him by his shoulder. My whole body was sparking from inside and yet I was calm. I couldn't see the face but the touch was familiar. My mind stung me with the thought of Siddharth.

Butterflies flapped their wings in my stomach.

My gaze stabilized and the clutch on my waist got tight. My other hand was in his hands too. It was Siddharth.

He was looking straight in my eyes with his black eyes. There was a moment of silence between us but it didn't feel empty. It's like we were talking through eyes. We didn't need words to understand each other. Then he broke the soothing silence.

"What happened? Why were you lost?"

"Um... I just... I came to know something."

I realized I am still in his sturdy hands. I jerked myself off from his clutch. I saw him trying to hide his smile behind his knuckles.

"What did you came to know?" He was still smiling.

"That Nikhil is the brother of Vijay uncle. That makes him my so-called uncle too! ....And he is an *ark* too!" He started grinning now.

"You knew it, didn't you?" I rested my hands on my waist and stared at him intensely.

He took a step back and showed his palms to me.

"Relax... I...I knew it but I was told not to tell you!"

"I am master's daughter, you could've told me!" I nearly screamed at him.

"In exchange, I can tell something else!" He was negotiating with me.

"What?"

"That— Shefali is a demon hunter. Crimson one!"

"What?"

"Yea." He patted my shoulder.

Why on earth I don't have a normal life and normal people around me?

Siddharth tapped onto my shoulders. "Um... Vijay sir told me to help you in pasting codes so..."

"Oh yea, Right!" I nearly forgot about that.

We hurriedly started the work and taped all the codes on the table. I was talking so much stuff without taking any breath and he was just listening. Soon all the codes were pasted and it was time to confront Nikhil.

We were walking towards the building. At the football ground I saw Nikhil with other boys playing a friendly match. My residual emotions came on surface and I ran to him.

He saw me and saw my face in the lights on the ground. He ran away too. I elevated my speed but no use, I could not compare myself to an *ark*!

"What? Why... are you chasing me?" He was still running away.

"Because... it's you! You... bastard!"

"What in the world I did something to own these respectful words?"

"You are an *ark*!" I shouted. No one could hear me because we were running at the corner.

He stopped with a jerk. I nearly crashed into him.

"What did you say?" His voice sounded serious.

"That you are an ark, I don't mind that but... you are my uncle!" My brows frowned.

"You don't mind that I am a demon hunter!"

I was not digesting that he is my uncle!

"You are talking like you didn't know anything. About me or the fact that I know about you people. The most disturbing thing is that... You... you are my uncle and I can't see you in that way. You will always be my stupid ass friend, that's it!" He laughed.

"Talk with respect! I am your uncle." He laughed again.

I smacked his head. He laughed again and hooked his hand around my neck. We walked back where Siddharth was standing.

"Everything settled?" He had his hands in his pockets.

"Yea...and we will always be friends." He patted my head. I gave him a look.

"But Sara, who told you? I was supposed to tell you." We were walking to building. Nikhil left his game.

"Your big brother did."

"Ah! I guess you know everything now."

"Yes." I was proud of myself.

We reached the building while teasing and chatting with each other.

"Alright! I am bit tired and have to wake up early so I gonna go now. Bye, goodnight! "

"Good night uncle!" I stuck my tongue out to tease him. He did the same.

"Well, tomorrow is the start of the event. We gotta wake up early. Good night!" Siddharth looked at me.

His gaze always felt something else. His eyes were warm. I always felt like they were asking a question to me and are curious about some answer.

"Yea."

I looked up in the sky. The moon was shimmering up. It seemed beautiful but today something was different about it. It looked more pretty than usual.

"The moon is lovely." I looked at him.

"I wish." He smiled and then left.

I didn't understand. What was it? 'I wish!' He could have said yes it is, bastard! My lovely bastard! I smiled to myself and ran to my room.

Next morning, the bus arrived from the sister school. We all cheered at their entrance. They also cheered back. Nikhil, Prashant, Shree, Daksha, Siddharth and I were standing in the mob. Parul was not there as her health has gone down. She had gotten much paler than before. I scolded her for not seeing the doctor. She said that she will definitely do it after the event and she needs rest so I left her in the room with all possible things she will be needed in absence.

The students got off from the bus and were escorted to their staying place. They ate with us at the dining hall. The event got started at early afternoon. All of us were in our uniforms for the marchpast. Our school did the marchpast and some welcoming dances were performed. After that a, friendly match of football took place. The whole school was excited as adrenaline rush kicked inside everyone. The match was cut throat. Best players of both school were in front of each other. Siddharth and Nikhil were also in the team.

The match was thrilling as sky ride. Till the end, it was not decided who will take the winner title. At the end, the sister school won.

After a short break, the principal sir delivered speech and announced the start of Annual joint event. We all were having fun but I was missing Parul. She was still in her room.

The break for snacks was announced. After filling our hungry stomach, we crashed on chairs.

"Where is Parul?" Shree seemed worried.

"She is not feeling good. She seems weak and she says that she needs rest."

"Hm."

He didn't say much. After the day when he confessed, Shree was never himself again. He was still in hope that one day, his happily ever after will come!

"Hey! Sara, we need to go. Other school is asking about the projects." I nodded and left others with Prashant.

All the projects got submitted and were marked in the list with assigned codes. It took an hour while other were still on break.

When we went back, volleyball match was on its peak. Soon I replaced the current setter in the team. This time, we won the game as our wing spikers were of different level.

The day was called off. Other important events will be held tomorrow and the rest of the day was given to tear off the exhaustion. The sun was up in the sky but was about to set. Everyone dragged their feet off the ground and merrily went to their rooms.

I fell on my bed for a while and dozed off without knowing. I jerked and opened my eyes suddenly as someone called my name. I looked around, there was no one and the sun was completely down. I looked at the clock. I slept for half an hour. I went to Parul's room to check on her. She was still sleeping so I didn't disturb her and came back to my room. My stomach growled so I went to the dining hall. Everyone was there.

"Sara! How is Parul now?" Shree was still worried.

"She was sleeping so I left her. This morning was the last I saw her standing."

"You know what? Drag her out of the room and make her breathe fresh air then she will feel alright." Prashant stole salad from my plate while saying this.

"He is right, we need to get her out." Shree supported him.

"Fine! And also she needs to have dinner." I slammed my palms at the table.

We chatted about other competitions in the events and soon our plates were empty. I ran to Parul's room and knocked on it. She didn't open it. I called her name several times, and finally she opened the door.

She looked fragile and too weak to stand. She was pale as someone sucked her blood out.

"Parul? Are you alright? You look... dead!" I was shocked to see her in this state.

"I am alright it's just..."

"You are suffering from severe jaundice! You are going to the hospital now and you are coming with me to eat something. I will not hear anything!" I was so mad at her for not taking care of herself.

"Fine." She said in a frail voice and smiled lightly.

She walked slowly with me to the dining hall. She only ate salad while we all watched her like a snow globe.

"What have you done to yourself?" Prashant was questioning and mocking her.

"Let her eat!" Shree glared at Prashant.

Prashant raised his hands in surrender. I looked at Nikhil. Nikhil was somewhat quiet.

Parul slowly ate her meal. Me and Prashant supported her and took her to the garden. A lot of students were strolling there.

"She should rest some more. Don't take her out." Nikhil was acting like an uncle.

"She will feel good once she walks a bit. She was in her room all day. Let her breathe." Prashant countered.

"Nikhil, let her go!" Shree grabbed his shoulder.

Nikhil stepped back and nodded.

"Nikhil, I want to talk about something!" Parul said in her feeble voice.

Nikhil nodded and they both walked to the corner of the garden. I could see a hint of jealousy on Shree's face. Prashant and I exchanged glances and giggled. We ran over to the other corner and tried to eavesdrop but failed. We didn't hear anything. After a while they came back to us. We acted like we didn't do anything. Meanwhile Aarya came and called Nikhil away.

"Shree, let's have a walk!" Parul pushed us into surprise.

Shree dropped his jaw on the ground and I could sense his spinning head.

"... Ye... yes, sure!" He stuttered.

Prashant and I were stunned. We froze where we stood. Shree helped Parul while walking and they walked on the main road of the campus. Prashant and I chased them secretly. They were talking about somethings. I could conclude some actions of surprise from Shree.

I couldn't figure out what they were talking about. Soon they stopped at a point, we were still looking at them. Shree took her hand, I could see that much from the street light. They were smiling at each other and then suddenly Shree crashed his lips onto Parul's.

I went crazy. We went crazy!

I couldn't speak anything and kept hitting Prashant. He was frozen at his place like his feet got stuck onto the ground. We looked at each other with our widened eyes. We ran to find Nikhil so we could tell him. Prashant nearly crashed into a wounded boy. His elbow was covered into blood. We ran here and there and finally to the building. We saw Nikhil, Siddharth, Daksha and Shefali there. Some other known faces were there.

"Shefali! What are you doing here?" Prashant couldn't control as he saw her.

"She can tell that later but Nikhil, you need to come and hear us!" I interrupted.

Suddenly we heard a shrill scream and then collective screaming. What was happening? Prashant and I peeked through the window but couldn't see anything. We all ran towards the ground but Siddharth clutched my hand.

"What?"

"I will tell you but right now listen to me!" I could not oppose him. He dragged me upstairs.

"Will you tell me now?" He broke the lock of the terrace.

"In a moment."

We went to the edge from where the whole ground was visible. I looked closely. A figure was there, giant as an elephant.

"What is that?" I couldn't figure it out.

"The time has come, you are going to see the Selene warrior!" He was tensed. I saw him drawing his sword from behind of his shirt.

His words shook me. As he said those words, a loud noise was heard. As I turned my head, my eyes could not believe. I could see the Selene warrior in front of me. I could see Kaumudi. I could see her. She was enormous, so enormous that she could wipe out everything in sight in one go. She was as enormous as thousand elephants together. Her hairs were waving in the air like an ocean wave. Her body had only red skin which were just muscles. Her jaw was kind of ripped and her eyes had hunger. Her knees were folded and hands were in front as she was about to sprint. I was scared, the ground beneath my feet had already vanished at her appearance. Suddenly she roared that made everyone shake from fear.

"How'd she..." I was having a hard time finding words.

"Parul! Kaumudi was inside her. She revived her, in reality, Parul was dead long ago!"

My brain stopped working. Parul? The girl who was my very good friend all these years, that Parul? That Parul who was worried for everyone? My breathing elevated, it seemed like I was having a panic attack for the first time in my life. I was frozen.

Suddenly Nikhil and Daksha with some other people came to the roof. They all had swords in their hands.

"Her roar... called their kind!" Nikhil was panting a bit.

"I could sense the presence of moon warriors!" Shefali too was with them. That guy with whom I did campus rounds on my birthday was there too. *Mind Blasting!*

"Her life is important! ...Nikhil, Daksha, Shefali and I will stay here and cover her. Tell the rest to go down and protect others. Once Mandraak appears, you all know what you have do!" Everyone dispersed at Siddharth's command.

He suddenly took my hand and put the squinx ring on my finger.

"Sara! I know it's difficult for you but I want you to summon Mandraak right now. We need him!" He rubbed the back of my hand.

I could hear the screams down. Parul was the Selene warrior all this time and... I don't know where Shree and Prashant are? My breaths were getting shorter.

"I know you can do this!" Siddharth said to me again.

"Consider this as your mission! Go for it Sara!" Nikhil held me by my shoulder.

I took a long breath. I already felt the sting of squinx ring and blood was oozing.

"I will do my best to save everyone!"

Siddharth took his stance with sword. His hilt was black with carvings of ocean waves and a dragon. I've seen these kinds of hilt in books but was seeing them in reality for the first time. He stood in front of me and something hit my mind, a familiar and blurry image of a silhouette. *A person with a sword.*

It could be my imagination, I jerked it off and sat in the meditation position.

I could hear them circling me. I closed my eyes but my brain was not calm, it was wandering. Screams were falling into my ears and shouting of demons and demon hunters, frequent roars of Kaumudi were audible. My mind was hovering over the fact that Parul her medium. Where Prashant and Shree are? Are they alright?

All these thoughts were hindering me to open root chakra, the lowest one. I need to stabilize my mind otherwise a lot of people will lose their life. Everyone's life is at stake in this gamble. I gathered my residual courage and slowly discarded every voice and thought. Root chakra got opened and gradually all the chakras were opened.

I, Sara, request Lord Mandraak to appear!

I wanted to feel that strong and ominous hiss over my head. There was nothing.

I tried again with intensified emotions and this time I felt huge wavering over my head. I knew I succeeded!

Mandraak's eyes got filled with rage as he saw the Kaumudi. Mandraak hissed loudly with his wide opened mouth, showing his enormous pair of fangs.

"Nikhil, you stay here and everyone we need to go down. Things are going to be rough down there." Siddharth commanded again.

I looked at him. I wanted him to stay close to me but he couldn't. He was a demon hunter, his first priority was saving others' lives. I wanted to blurt at that moment that I liked him a lot and maybe loved him but only my eyes spoke. I failed saying anything to him but I wanted him to return, alive.

"Come back soon!" I could only say that.

"Sure!" After saying this he jumped down the building.

"Sara! You did a great job summoning Mandraak and now I want you to get all the students away from the school. Get the place evacuated and... please be safe! Here, take this and use it. I want to see my friend and my niece to be alive after this. Let's go!" Nikhil handed me a small and sharp arming sword.

As I took it, I had the confidence that I could handle it too and I accepted everything as it was. My top priority was to save other students around. *I belong to the clan of demon hunters!*

Nikhil smiled and rushed with me down the stairs. We went to the ground and the sight was horrible. Demons were everywhere and were chasing students. Nikhil ran and aimed for their neck. One slash was enough to perish them away.

Nikhil went slashing heads of demons there while I waved at everyone to follow me. I told them to run away from the school to the mountain area. Some students from our school took the lead and ran away with everyone. I could see a lot of hunters fighting with demons. I could spot Siddharth fighting with one on the first floor of the school building. The half building of the school had already been demolished and some students were still running in the unharmed portion of the building.

Mandraak and the Kaumudi were fighting. Mandraak was spitting poison over her while she was scratching his neck. There was so much tension in the air. For a moment I thought that all this could turn into a nightmare and when I wake up, everything fades away but some corpses made me realize that it's not a dream. I called for Nikhil and pointed at the building where students were running. He did a sprint and I was behind him.

"Everyone! Get out and run to the mountain nearby!" I shouted with every inch of my strength and then I realized that there were demons too. Nikhil flipped his sword and joined back with me.

"Sara! If anything happens, always remember that you were the best person in my life and I am sorry for putting you in this position!" Then he started slicing heads.

I saw demons coming towards me. They were hideous, I was terrified. They stretched their arms towards me and then… they couldn't reach me.

"No one dares to touch my daughter with those filthy hands!"

"Master!" I exclaimed. If everything was right that time, I would've laughed for calling him that!

"Take everyone away and keep your guard up! Don't forget whose daughter you are. I will handle it here."

Master and Nikhil were fighting while I took everyone and ran away to the mountain.

After leaving everyone at the mountain, I came back to the school. Mandraak was still fighting with Kaumudi. They were coiled with each other. I looked around for familiar faces. Daksha was fighting in one but she was in bad shape. She was injured but she was giving her everything and— same with everyone. Siddharth was a bit more badly injured than the rest. It became quite stable on the ground as the master reached. He was the master for a reason. I need to find Shree and Prashant.

Suddenly I heard a growl and as I turned, I saw a demon. He stretched his hand to catch me but I duck down. I got a scratch on my forehead because of his pointed claws. I fell on the ground and caressed my wound. The demon came and grabbed me by my neck and raised me up. My feet were struggling for the ground and my throat was struggling for air.

I was getting strangled.

I tried to free myself from his clutch but couldn't. I tried to reach my sword but the struggle of air overpowered me. I prayed to God to save and then I heard Siddharth calling my name. He jumped and slashed that demon's hand. The neck was released and a wave of oxygen hit my throat, I coughed. As I raised my eyes, I saw the demon's head rolling on the ground, Siddharth killed him.

"Are you alright?" He took my face in his hands and looked at my forehead cut.

"Yes I am, are you?"

I looked at him. His forehead was scratched and blood was oozing from his shoulder and hands. He looked somewhat tired.

"I am alright! Find a place to hide." He stood me up.

"I need to find Prashant and Shree!"

"Where is Nikhil? Why is he not with you?"

"I don't know. Master came for the rescue. I led students to the mountain." We were jogging across the ground. He saw my arming sword.

"Fine! Look for them but don't get pointed out and use the sword, it will definitely help... just don't die!" The situations had put him in tight spot.

As said this he looked into my eyes and hugged me tightly as I was slipping away. I was about to hug him back but he left and ran away.

I took a breath and paced slowly around to look for them. I couldn't find them but then I heard someone in pain. I ran behind the wall and saw Shree sitting against the wall.

"Shree!" I ran to him.

"Sara!" He was covered in blood. His hand looked crashed and blood was flowing continuously out of it. His leg seemed twisted or fractured too.

"Are you alright?"

"Sara! Parul!" He was fighting for his breaths.

"I know and you need to get out of here! Where is Prashant?"

"He ...at the mountain, he took everyone with him. Now...listen, Parul...she gave a responsibility of her last wish! She told me to kill her once the demon perishes. If she... not killed then the demon... is able to revive herself through her." His sentences were breaking.

"What the hell?"

"So... listen! I want you... to take me to Parul... to kill her. I must do that because I cannot be saved now! My legs are... fractured and I have already lost a lot of blood. My organs... has ruptured too. This is my last wish to you! ...Please! "

"How can I let you die?" Tears were streaming down my face.

"It's okay Sara! It's just a cruel fate. We eventually had to through this!" I sat near him.

"Thank you!" He took a breath and I was crying.

"Do you know... that in eleventh class I tried... to confess my feelings... to her by writing 'Isn't the moon lovely? ' on the paper?" He laughed.

"What does that phrase mean?" I wiped my tears.

"I love you!" His eyes were closing a bit.

A heart skipped a beat. That's what he meant all this time. Siddharth was trying to confess his love to me.

"And she didn't understand! But Sara...I want you... to find... love and be happy, forever and... become the... best pilot!" He smiled again.

I looked at him, cursing destiny and this cruel fate. We are kids who didn't even pass our school out and yet we have to bear through this.

"Lend me... your shoulder." I gave him support and took all his weight over me. He was severely injured.

I dragged him behind of the wall and saw the terrific sight. Mandraak was injured too but the Kaumudi's neck was between his fangs and she was yelling in pain. The master was also there and hundreds of other students too, all were covered in blood. They all were demon hunters who were studying in our school.

They all clapped their hands with index fingers folded inwards and screamed in unison.

"Atmokinesis! First form, rising sun!" And banged on the ground with both palms.

Atmokinesis, the method of manipulating the weather using physic abilities! I was about to witness something that no one had seen in centuries. I only read about this in books.

I was watching closely, every demon hunter was kneeled on the ground. It was like they were sending some energy to the ground. Mandraak was struggling holding her neck and Kaumudi warrior was scratching his skin away.

In the next few minutes, the sun rose up in the middle of the night. I knew that it was about to be midnight but I could see the sunrise in front of my eyes. As the sun rays hit the Kaumudi's skin, her body started to turn to ashes. She screamed loudly, so loudly that it could cause a storm in the air. Soon her whole body turned to ashes.

The master jumped and caught the falling body of Parul. She was lifeless, I could sense but didn't want to accept. Shree and I walked slowly to Parul's body and suddenly Shree threw his body over her.

The sword pierced them, at once.

Before I could understand anything, it happened. I froze, Parul and completely dead. The sword was through here heart.

I lost senses and fell onto the ground. Siddharth came to hold me. Shree spit blood out of his mouth and then before I knew, he took his last breath and stopped breathing. It happened so fast that I couldn't even say or understand anything.

I screamed, loudly! I cried with everything I had! My friends were laying in front of me, dead! It felt like I lost everything. I just looked at them, I couldn't do anything. I cannot bring them back to life! Master came to calm me down but I was not myself! Before I could cry one more tear, I felt a jerk on my neck and darkness crept in front of my eyes.

My eyelids felt heavy, light fell onto my eyes— and I slowly opened them and looked around. Nikhil and Prashant were beside my bed. Nikhil had bandages all over. He looked exhausted. I was in a room of a half destroyed building. I looked outside of the window, the sun was up and then everything flashed before my eyes.

My eyes welled up again as the thought of Parul and Shree occurred. They are dead now!

"Are you alright?" Nikhil held me by my shoulder.

"You think?"

He took a long breath and pulled something out from his pocket. A piece of paper, looked like a letter and handed it to me.

"This is from Parul." Then he left.

I opened the letter with tears in my eyes.

Hey! Don't cry. I know the time when you get this, I will be gone. I knew my fate, I knew that the demon was inside me and that demon made me kill those students and I am sorry for that. I never remembered doing that. The demon inside me had tortured me a lot for the killings. I beared till the last limit but...I will lose, I know! Actually I was dead in the car accident when I lost my family but that demon took my body and revived me and herself but thanks to that, I was able to meet you! You were an important part of my life and Siddharth is a good guy, you both will make a good couple. Siddharth knows about me. We've already confronted each other about this. I wanted to do a good thing before dying so I want you to find your love for him. I didn't know about Shree but when he confessed, I was happy but I didn't want to hurt him so I didn't accept him. I will tell him my real identity so he could hate me and save himself! Sara, you were my soul sister! I wish you achieve your dream and find happiness in this world. Please be happy for me once I am gone. I will be relived from torture of this demon. Look for me in the sky. I will be the leftmost star!

PS- I will be waiting for you in the heaven, if I am there!

I closed my eyes, I lost another friend after Mahi! I must label myself as bad luck! Master came to me.

"Are you alright?"

I nodded. He gloved my hand.

"Look, this is a painful reality of this world. Take your time for grief but don't take much time because it will not snuggle along with you. It will keep moving and then you will lose other important things."

I looked at him, he was radiating from the fatherly glow. He was calm. He surely have scars on his heart, similar to mine. His experience was saying these words and somewhere he was right too. No one can outrun destiny's game plan. I smiled heavily at him.

I looked at Prashant, he had a letter too in his hands. He looked devastated.

"It's alright! No one could've stopped it." He nodded.

I knew he was crying.

"Um...Sara!" Master said.

"Yes"

"Would you like to come to your house?" I knew what he meant.

"Ah... I... I will return to the place where my dadi is waiting for her Bittu! I cannot leave her but I'll visit my house too! "

He smiled. "You are my pride! That's what I had expected, you are just like your mother but don't forget about your this father!" He grinned and wiped my tears away.

"I should head back. I need to fulfil my duty as the master!" He kissed my forehead and went away. I looked at Prashant.

"Prashant!"

"I am fine, but I wonder that in absence of that rascal, with whom I am going to bicker!"

He stood up and hugged me. I knew he was sad but his mental strength was his biggest strength. He accepted everything.

I stood up, the squinx ring was still in my finger. I wondered if Mandraak was still wavering here.

"Where is Siddharth?"

"He must be outside." Prashant collected himself.

I walked outside and looked around. Everything was destroyed, the whole school had turned into debris. The oak tree also got broken. Only the junior section building was there in which we all took shelter. I scanned through each room. Wounded were getting treated. I saw Daksha and Shefali on bed, they were wrapped in bandages too. A lot of other students were there too. In another room, other students were sitting on the ground and some were sleeping. There was a relief after seeing them. I was looking for him but couldn't find him. I climbed the stairs to the roof. I saw him standing at the edge. He was looking far. He was also in bandages. I walked to him and stood beside him.

"Are you okay?" He didn't flinch.

"Yes... ha! Trying to be. How are you?"

"A bit relieved and scared!" My heart beats were elevating.

"Me too!"

"Where is Mandraak?"

"After you passed out, he left too. He knew that his part was done." His voice seemed heavy.

"How's your wound?" I forgot that I had a scar on my forehead.

"It's good...how's your hand?"

"Stop worrying about my hand and worry about me! I was dead scared that I might lose you in this fight. I was scared that what if you didn't wake up? What if I didn't make it out? When your forehead got scarred, I wanted to scream! Do you understand how much I was worried about you?" I was in his clutch. Blood was coming out of his scars.

I didn't say anything, I just looked at him.

His eyes had worry which turned into slight anger. His voice was low but echoing. He didn't want to hurt me but also didn't know how to say things. He doesn't know how to express his intense emotions!

"You won't admit directly, will you?" I didn't blink.

"Wh— what?" He let me go. His stuttering words were enough proof.

"Fine, I'll do it." I fixed my gaze at him.

"Siddharth, I know the meaning of the words that you spoke earlier."

His eyes shone bright and he turned to me.

"I liked you for a long time, when...I don't know? But now I know that I loved you. I love you, Siddharth!" He was in shock. He gathered himself.

"I know I tried to confess to you a couple of times but I was sad that you didn't get my words. I thought you don't like me at all...Sara! You were never a non-existent person for me. You were the most existing person for me ever. You are my thoughts and my dreams and now I can't imagine my life without you... I love you! From now on, I am going to be yours, forever!"

"Forever?"

He slowly came closer to me and landed a soft kiss on my cheek. With a slight smile, I hugged him. He wrapped me in his arms and sniffed my hair. The gardens started to grow inside me, again but this time— flowers of the garden bloomed too.

He leaned his forehead against mine.

"Forever yours!"

A slight smile popped onto my face. His warmth wrapped me. I wanted to stay like that forever!

He was the bastard whom I loved madly!

It's been two years now. We all passed out of school and now we are studying in the university. The rules and regulations were very strict here.

After the incident at school, the school was rebuilt in the next six months and now it is brand new.

At the event, I later came to know that a huge number of demon hunters were from sister school so the situation was handled. There were around other hundred warriors who were under Siddharth.

Siddharth and I have a relationship of two years old. In this we dated and tried to understand each other more. He has started to look more handsome than before. He told me many weird and new things. We went exploring many different places together. He still likes my craziness.

Dadi and I kept a promise that we will never reveal anything to Mumma or Papa. I visited the south mountains a couple of times with Siddharth. Master was happy to see me there.

Prashant confessed to Shefali too. Prashant and Shefali are also together now. They gave themselves a chance. Surprisingly, Shefali knew about Prashant. They have been together for like a year and a half.

Aarya got admitted in other defence university but she is still in touch.

Nikhil and Daksha were also with us. Nikhil is still playing the role of my uncle!

After the death of Selene warrior, the number of demons have gone down but they are still out there, somewhere so they have the priority of being a demon hunter and saving the human kind.

Memorial of Shree, Parul and Mahi were laid side by side at the hometown. Whenever I visited dadi, I go there to tell them about my whereabouts.

Every night, I look up to the sky and find the leftmost star twinkling. I know Parul was up there and looking at me and beside her, Shree is also there to take care of her but the thought of them not being here stabs me, always. I wonder how things would've been if they were here right now? But I have accepted everything. I pray that they are happy in their afterlife.

I am happy that all this happened because if this didn't happen then I never would have met Parul, one of the best person in my life and Siddharth, the love of my life. I know that he is the only person with whom I am willing to spend the rest of my life with!

In every universe!

Because he is only high class bastard to whom I could love.

Dear reader,

Thank you so much for reading my story. This story was written two years ago but I couldn't publish it back then, reasons!

I am writing this to cheer you up.

DON'T GIVE UP!

KEEP BELIVING!

IT'LL BE OKAY!

Things can be rough sometimes but it's all going to be okay in the end. Just believe in yourself.

It's not necessary that we'll do the right thing always. We all are allowed to make mistakes.

In reality, this world doesn't do justice to anyone so don't stress too much. Remember, you can take a break and be you.

Well, I will be very happy if you send me your photograph with this book. I'll make sure to post it on my insta ☺!

Remember, make yourself happy. Be you!

www.ingramcontent.com/pod-product-compliance
Lightning Source LLC
Chambersburg PA
CBHW021439150726
47989CB00001B/313